CONFESSIONS
OF A BOYFRIEND
STEALER

CONFESSIONS

OF A BOYFRIEND

STEALER

[A BLOG]

robynn clairday

DELACORTE PRESS

Published by
Delacorte Press
an imprint of
Random House Children's Books
a division of Random House, Inc.
New York

Visit us on the Web! www.randomhouse.com/teens
Educators and librarians, for a variety of teaching tools, visit us at
www.randomhouse.com/teachers

Library of Congress Cataloging-in-Publication Data
Clairday, Robynn.
Confessions of a boyfriend stealer / Robynn Clairday.
p. cm.
Summary: Florida high school junior and aspiring documentary film-
maker Genesis Bell's blog tells the true story of the unbelievable events
that caused the breakup of her friendship with her two best friends.
ISBN 0-385-73242-2 (trade) — ISBN 0-385-90267-0 (glb)
[1. Weblogs—Fiction. 2. High schools—Fiction. 3. Interpersonal
relations—Fiction. 4. Dating (Social customs)—Fiction.
5. Documentary films—Fiction. 6. Family life—Florida—Fiction.
7. Schools—Fiction. 8. Florida—Fiction.] I. Title.
PZ7.C526Co 2005
[Fic]—dc22
2004022969

The text of this book is set in 12-point Minion.

Book design by Angela Carlino

Printed in the United States of America

September 2005

10 9 8 7 6 5 4 3 2 1

BVG

acknowledgments

I'd like to thank Melyssa Reisler Cooke and Michelle Churchman for being such faithful, patient, and steadfast readers. I'd like to thank my morning crew, who were always willing to offer goodwill, support, and encouragement: Wendy, Jody, and Rachel from Starbucks; Deb from Manhattan Bagel; and Mary and Carl from Country Kettle and Oven.

I'd also like to extend my sincere appreciation and gratitude to Michelle Poploff and Joe Cooper, whose guidance, enthusiasm, and knowledge were crucial during the entire editorial process.

I'd like to thank Matt, as always, for everything.

CONFESSIONS
OF A BOYFRIEND
STEALER

MOST RECENT ENTRIES CALENDAR
VIEW FRIENDS LINKS PHOTOS

Confessions of a Boyfriend Stealer—
Blog by Genesis Bell

Behind the Confessional Curtain
[All About Me!]

BIRTHDAY: June 8—Gemini, the twins. I don't think I have a dual personality, unless one is keeping quiet.
AGE: 16½
FAVORITE FOOD(S): Tacos, pizza, IHOP waffles, ice cream, M&M's, and KFC. I am a total health nut. Right.
LOVE: Means never tattooing a guy's name on your butt. (But if he wants to tattoo mine on his, I'm cool with it.) ☺
FAVORITE MUSIC: Alternative, emo, techno, rock, and rap. Some headbanger stuff. My tastes fluctuate with my moods. I don't often follow the trends. Currently love Headlock, Zara, and Dis. Mainstream like Missy Elliot and Ludacris. Getting a little interested in

1

old stuff like Nirvana and Ozzy (loved his documentary too).

Favorite graffiti: I saw this in a bathroom once and it stuck in my head. It's so classy (not). *Everywhere I am, all eyes are on me. I guess that's why it's so hard for me to pee.*

Favorite movie: *The Blair Witch Project, Scream* (1 & 2), and *Buffy the Vampire Slayer* (the TV version was better, but the movie is funky).

Favorite TV: Documentaries (like *Living in New York City, The Farmer's Wife, A Dog's World*) and reality shows (like *The Real World, The Bachelor, American Idol*) and old stuff like *The Brady Bunch.*

Family Life: Basically dysfunctional. Some would say borderline trailer trash, but never to my mother's face!

Worst Moment: What happened about two months ago!

Best Moment: What happened about two months ago (I'm not trying to be cute or mystical, I swear)! You'll see.

Pets: I wish. When I'm running my own life, I'll have a dog or two or ten.

Favorite Color: Purple.

Dream: To finally, finally kick CJ's ass . . . I'm kidding. To produce totally awesome but original television, particularly reality shows and documentaries.

Philosophy: No one here gets out alive. (Jim Morrison, the Doors)

Favorite Links

www.coca-cola.com

www.ihop.com

www.m-ms.com

www.zara-music.com

www.nirvanaweb.com

www.seeklyrics.com/lyrics/enigma

www.blairwitch.com

www.mtv.com/onair/osbournes

Confessions of a Boyfriend Stealer—Blog by Genesis Bell

[1ST ENTRY]

I *just* found out that CJ Thompson, my ex–best friend, is going to write a blog, and more important, she is going to use it to totally and completely trash me. (Several people came up to me in school to warn me about CJ's plans.) I know she'll be cranking out megalies and megacrap about what happened two months ago. No one's more bloodthirsty than Miss Anorexica when she's on the warpath.

But that's her. I won't stoop to her level, no matter how tempting (or easy) it would be!

I've got to tell my side, or people might actually believe my ex–best friend's lies. I guess I'd better tell the whole story, background info and all.

See, my problem really was that I was just too vanilla nice. You would know me back then if you saw me. I was the cute-enough girl (cute, but not so cute as to be a threat to you or your friends). Think Jan Brady (www.hissandpop.com/celebrities/p/eveplumb) from *The Brady Bunch* but without the annoying personality and the whiny voice.

I was *so* Miss Supersupportive. I was the one who soothed CJ and Tasha during their "fat" moments (they're both twigs). I was the one who carried a spare tube of cover-up in my purse for their hickey emergencies. I was the one who comforted their male love slaves when things got too emotional and messy and CJ and Tasha didn't want to be bothered.

Don't think I'm some saint, though. After hearing my story, you'll realize that martyrdom is so not me.

I did it all because Tasha Dombrowski, CJ Thompson, and I were best friends. Just to be clear, we were not into modern-day chick bonding stuff. We didn't hug and cry. We didn't say we loved (or *luved*) each other. We didn't expect a lot of Oprah moments from our friendship.

We called ourselves the Terrible Three, which we eventually shortened to just the Terribles. If CJ or Tasha wanted a guy, she got him, no regrets, no remorse. I aided and abetted (yeah, yeah, I know. I was the Jan Brady Terrible, but I was still a Terrible). I defended CJ and Tasha, claiming it wasn't their fault that they were irresistible to every guy on the planet. I was always on rumor patrol, which meant trying to kill all gossip about the other Terribles (like the perpetual stories about CJ's being pregnant or Tash's having an STD).

We ruled. We weren't like the other kids. We were above it all. We were so beyond Jamaica Plains High.

Okay, so they got all the boyfriends while I watched from the sidelines, but it didn't bother me.

CJ and Tasha said I was a late bloomer when it came to guys and that maybe I'd attract them when I was older, like after high school. Some girls were just born with that late-bloomer gene, they said. I thought they were right—that I'd have to wait till later for the good stuff.

As it turned out, we were all three wrong.

CJ, Tasha, and I always swore that we'd be tight for life. It seemed believable for a long while.

At least to me.

The thing is, Tasha and CJ took me under their wing when I was new. I was just kind of floating around, which is typical for junior high schools when you're not instant clique material. Which means you don't fit in anywhere. And it was amazing, because Tasha and CJ were totally beautiful, not desperate, pathetic types latching onto the new kid.

Months later, I learned that there were girls who had formed actual We-Hate-Tasha-and-CJ chat rooms and that there wasn't a single girl in school who would be friends with either of them, but by then, I was like so what. By then, I was a full-fledged Terrible.

I'd moved to Jamaica Plains, Florida, three years before, and at first, the kids in middle school thought I was cool because I'd moved from California, but that wore off quickly once they found out I didn't know any big movie stars. It didn't take them long to pretty much forget I existed. I was too used to blending into the background.

The fact is that up until then I'd never really had a best friend. We moved around California a lot when I was a kid because my mother was always switching jobs and men. I think she got tired of it and that's why we've been in Jamaica Plains for so long; also, a psychic told her that Florida would be luckier for her.

When I was younger and lived in California, I spent a lot of time babysitting and watching TV. I had the most fun creating my own talk shows. I'd write out pages and pages of scripts filled with questions I'd ask celebrities and the smartass comments I'd make. I'd even throw in audience comments.

I've always wanted my own TV show, so maybe I'm like my father. He's a big producer of funky, famous documentaries. He's rich and successful. He moved to Toronto about ten years ago. Maybe I'll be rich some-day too. . . .

Anyway, back to the story. Back to what it meant to be a Terrible. It was all very cool. When anyone invited CJ and Tasha somewhere, the two of them would auto-matically assume I was included. Tasha or CJ would say something like, "Yeah, the three of us are going to Mac's party Saturday," even if Mac hadn't actually in-vited me. Soon people just expected me to show up at their parties. Tasha and CJ made sure that I was some-body in Jamaica Plains. I became a Terrible.

After a while, though, CJ and Tasha came to know me so well that they didn't even see me.

I didn't realize until a few months ago just how much they didn't see me, and how that would basically ruin everything. Being a sidekick has its disadvantages.

I was molded into this Jan Brady role practically from birth. My mother, Angela Bell, and my sister, Shay Bell, are pros when it comes to the world of male-female drama. However, they are not pros at taking care of bills or handling nasty phone calls from bill collectors or calling repair guys to come fix a leaky toilet or a zoinked-out refrigerator. That's where I come in. Angela found out early on that I'm *not* the type to fit into the Angela-Shay club (one really pathetic childhood memory to come later), so that meant I had to do something else.

I also try to keep things in our house under control. I guess in the Bell household I'm like the bouncer who doesn't like to mix with the customers too much but who still has to keep an eye on them.

Shay's motto is "Men are resources," and resources, of course, must be exploited or they go to waste. Shay could have gone to college instead of bartender school, but she's too restless and impatient for academics. She's changed bars a lot, but she's now working at the Post.

My mother's motto is "Get it while you can." And believe me, she does. Angela Bell isn't shy about going after what she wants. She figures that her job as a hairstylist offers only so many options, so why shouldn't she look elsewhere for satisfaction? By elsewhere, she means men, of course. She also likes to remind Shay and me that a female's shelf life is only so long, even with the benefit of implants and eye jobs.

I can't be a total hypocrite. We've lived a better life because Angela's and Shay's men have subsidized our family income, which means sometimes we can afford extras like expensive clothes and jewelry, which my mom and sister enjoy, and a really decent PC, which I appreciate. Alimony checks from my father and Shay's help too; Angela is also getting child support checks for me. All of it means we can live in nicer neighborhoods and drive fancier cars. If we relied strictly on my mom's and Shay's incomes, we'd barely be middle class. So, whatever. It's not as if I have to be like my mom and sister.

You're probably thinking that with a name like Genesis I should have been raised in some Bible-thumping, goody-goody family with a mom and dad, a dog named Spot, and the whole bit. The truth is, my mom had a stripper friend who called herself Genesis. She liked the irony. You know, dancer with a cross and all that. As if it hadn't been done to death by Madonna.

Angela says my own father, the long-gone James Robert, was the real deal—a real high-flying winner. I should be proud, I guess, because Shay's dad, Jeb Ryan, was just a plain old loser who was posing as a player.

My mother has a real thing for Southern boys. Bell is my mother's maiden name. She doesn't want us to have three different last names and look like trailer trash, so Shay and I use Bell too. We really don't see much of Jeb Ryan or James Robert, except for my father's child support checks and alimony from both of them.

I'd like to think I've been so traumatized by my bizzaro family that I lost interest in normal, romantic relationships, but that wasn't the case. I was just too comfy blending into the wallpaper.

But that all changed junior year, during the holiday break, the day after New Year's Day.

I'll tell you how it all began. Maybe you can figure out *why* it did.

It was Christmas break, and I'd spent most of my time eating way too much candy, sleeping in till noon, and trying to decide what I wanted my final media project to be about. My first project had been a fifteen-minute soap-opera spoof called *Alien Love,* which I had written and produced in the fall. I'd used theater geeks as the actors, since I, like everyone else in media lab, was into directing, producing, and doing behind-the-camera stuff. Not that we had any real studio equipment. Our school is so cheap that students have to bring their own camcorders. We also had cardboard cutouts of technical equipment instead of the real deal. We were supposed to use our *imagination.* Yeah, I'm not lying—cardboard cutouts of lighting and sound equipment. Can you see how pathetic our school is?

I'm just lucky my father sent me a really nice Sony camcorder (www.sonystyle.com) last year for my birthday; at least I could produce a higher-quality project.

Anyway, most of the kids in class had produced heavy, artsy stuff, mostly in black-and-white. You know the kind of movies I'm talking about. Five minutes of a seagull picking through the garbage or a kid in mime makeup chasing a balloon with weird music in the background. *Alien Love* was very different. I'd been sure that Mr. Nichols, our teacher, would hate my movie and love the highbrow flicks. But he totally shocked me by announcing that *Alien Love* was "brilliant and ironic." Which is really funny, when you realize how unacademic I am (except for media lab, I'm such a C student).

I'd been trying to figure out how to turn the fifteen-minute *Alien Love* into an hour-long show, but my mind kept wandering. I'd been imagining it was me instead of the alien girl who was being pursued by several gorgeous guys. My favorite fantasy scene involved a soulful-eyed babe, a hot tub, rose petals, and moonlight.

For a late bloomer, I have a very active imagination. Maybe I've watched too much WB and Fox.

But the day after New Year's, I was taking a break from my project. I was channel surfing and drinking Jolt cola, which can get you really wired. I settled for the Discovery Channel (www.discovery.com), because nothing else was on but reruns. Even MTV (www.mtv.com) had some marathon of really old

Real Worlds. I ended up watching this documentary about doctors in an emergency room. The blood and surgery scenes were gross, but I love shows about real life. I'll watch almost anything—from totally cheesy reality shows to totally brainiac documentaries. I just wish there were more programs about stuff I'm interested in. Something about real teen life, the real deal on high school. Something deep but fun too. If only . . .

Message Board

✉ **Just read genesis's first blog—I wonder—JUICYFRUIT45—at 10:39 a.m.**
Did anyone else read it? (:-o I wonder if genesis **really** stole her friends' men, or if the title is just a joke. i'm a sophomore at redwood high, so I don't know anyone at Jamaica plains, but I know girls like CJ and Tasha who think they are so hot. Ugh. >:-p

✉ **Re: Just read genesis's first blog—I wonder—QueenSheba—at 1:22 p.m.**
i am from Jamaica plains, but i am a sophomore so i don't really know the juniors well. plus, i'm more shy, and plus, our school is so big that it's easy to live in different worlds from other people. I can tell you that cj and Tasha are really popular, but they don't talk to sophomores. i've seen genesis around, and she seems nice. but i heard her friends totally dropped her because she did some stuff with their guys and

that is WRONG! no matter what. does anyone else agree?

✉ Re: Just read genesis's First Blog—I wonder—007ugo—at 9:12 p.m.

I don't agree at all! I'm from Jamaica Plains too, but I'm a senior. CJ and Tasha deserve whatever they get. They are super b#$ches! Trust me! I don't know them personally at all, but I've seen how they are. Ugh! I've heard rumors about genesis too, though I don't know her either. Just have seen her in the halls. Gossip is so untrustworthy! I think we should hear what Genesis has to say. I want to be fair. Anyway, I like the same music she does. Ozzy rules! ☺

MOST RECENT ENTRIES   CALENDAR
VIEW FRIENDS   LINKS   PHOTOS

28/03 02:27:52

Confessions of a Boyfriend Stealer—
Blog by Genesis Bell

[2ND ENTRY]

Omigod, I should have known. The rumors you've heard are all wrong. You'll get the real deal here. I realize I'm not someone who can write for hours at a time. I get tired of typing after a while, so this confession could take a few days. Stay with me, okay?

← →

Anyway, I turned off the doctor show and jumped to my feet, grinning. I knew what I wanted to do. Omigod! It was awesome. I would produce my own documentary. A true Genesis Bell Creation. My show would not only be *about* high school kids, but it would also be produced *by* a real live high school kid— me. I'd show the world what the teen perspective really was.

Mr. Nichols has been telling me that I have a real

flair for camerawork, and that I'm part of the new wave of creative minds who will take TV programming to new levels. Maybe he's right.

My first hour-long show was going to be amazing. I just had to figure out the details. Obviously, it had to be teen related . . . but about what specifically . . . ?

I was pacing around the living room when it hit me. Let's get this straight: you'll never catch me squealing and jumping up and down like certain ass cheerleaders do, but I was tempted, because I had just had the most awesome idea of all ideas. I was so psyched!

I was going to produce a Fiesta Beach documentary. Fiesta Beach is this party that the juniors and seniors throw every year around the end of January. A few select sophomores are allowed to go too. The party is always held at a house where the parents are away. There's always sand on the floor, blow-up palm trees, a limbo contest (limbo is a huge part of the party), and tiki torches, and everyone wears their bathing suit. They always play Latin and Jamaican music. Officially, the party is alcohol free, but in reality, people spike the punch (traditionally a mix of lime and orange juice) like crazy. It's really great because outside it's cold and gross, and inside you're pretending it's summer and you're on the beach. (Unfortunately, Jamaica Plains is four hours away from the nearest desirable beach. Oh, and four hours away from Disney too. We are the one place in Florida that no one ever wants to visit.)

The main thing about Fiesta Beach is that all the really important stuff happens at it. It's even bigger than the prom. Major hookups and breakups go down. This is where reps are made and unmade. There's usually a fight or two, between girls or guys. People end up talking about the party for the rest of the year. Last year, I spent most of the night keeping CJ and Tasha from getting their asses kicked by a couple of jealous girls from an out-of-town, tougher high school.

Some of the Fiesta Beaches have become legends.

Everyone would love being on a real TV show, which I was going to make sure would be very professional and very cool. Man, I was dying to share my brilliant brainstorm with someone.

But Tasha was in Colorado skiing with her family, and CJ was in Cancún with her two cousins, staying in some ritzy condo. I hate the snow, and I don't get along with CJ's superbitchy cousins (who unfortunately own the ritzy condo), so I decided to stay home. Shay was in the Caribbean with one of her guys; she didn't invite me along. No surprise. My mother was party-hopping every night and shopping every day. She didn't invite me to do either—thank God.

Angela, Shay, and I are okay as long as we each do our own thing. I keep my school life totally separate from my home life. Angela and my sister have met CJ and Tasha a few times, but they barely know them, and vice versa. Which is cool with me.

I tried IMing Tasha and CJ but didn't hear back from either of them. No big surprise there either. Tasha is impossible to reach when she's skiing (I think she goes into some sort of weird skier's trance as soon as she hits the slopes). CJ had only IM'd me twice to let me know she and her cousins had met tons of hot guys and were partying their asses off in Cancún. Maybe it would be better to tell the Terribles about Fiesta Beach in person anyway.

I think CJ and Tash would be pretty psyched about the show idea, especially if it meant they might get a lot of close-ups. They'd probably want DVD copies.

Which got me thinking. I'd have to come up with a theme or an angle for my documentary. Mr. Nichols said every documentary has an underlying message. CJ and Tash could help me. Maybe my angle would be *The Terribles at Fiesta Beach.* The three of us could be the main characters, and the show could be about our experiences at the party. It would be really personal but honest. I grinned. And we could end up big stars. Yeah, I was delusional, I admit it.

I finally calmed down and found some scrap paper under a pile of paid bills (electric, rent, cell, all stamped and ready to go) on the coffee table. I jotted down *Fiesta Beach—Through the Eyes of the Terrible Three.* Corny. I scratched that out. If this was going to be a show about the Terribles, I'd have to be careful to make it objective and scientific, like a professional documentary. I'd have to be careful not to make it some lovefest about me, CJ, and Tasha. It could get tricky. I wrote *The True Terrible Fiesta Beach Story* and immediately crossed that out. I frowned and folded up the paper. Of course, I hadn't made a final decision on anything yet. Mr. Nichols says producers have to go through lots of changes before settling on the end product. And I really had to get serious about figuring out all the fancy features on my camcorder. I'd only used a few for *Alien Love,* but there were tons of special effects that could make the documentary awesome. Ugh, that meant reading the manual.

I realized I had 126 hours to go before break was over and I could start talking to everyone at school about my show.

My thoughts were interrupted by a sudden monstrous growling. It was my stomach.

Obviously, I needed some nourishment after working my brain so hard. I went into the kitchen for my favorite snack, Doritos (www.doritos.com) and M&M's (www.m-ms.com). I know it sounds like a gaggy combo but it's surprisingly good. I mixed the two in a big bowl and pulled a Coke out of the fridge. Sometimes pigging out is really good for you—I think the body needs regular doses of junk food. Keeps you real. I'd just popped an M&M into my mouth when the phone rang.

I grabbed the cordless and almost choked on the M&M when I heard the voice on the other end. Nick Pilates. CJ's guy. They'd been on-again, off-again for a year. He was okay. Very cute, but he seemed kind of dim to me. Not that we talked much. Unlike CJ's other guys, he hadn't needed me to run interference or referee. Tasha's newest boyfriend, Chi Nguyen, however, had. Chi is adorable. Vietnamese American. And he's rich. But he was horribly insecure. Tasha was the worst person in the world for him, but he was so whipped that it was almost scary. At peak insecurity points, Chi IM'd me ten times a day. It was always Tasha this and Tasha that. Pathetic. Chi was visiting family in California while Tasha was skiing on Mount Big Poop or whatever, so I was Chi free for a while.

Nick goes, "Hey, Gen, what's up?" He sounded as if we talk every day.

I was so stunned that I stammered something stupid like "Uh, nothing, really. Eating, I guess." I coughed. The M&M had irritated my throat.

The next thing I knew he was asking if he could stop by. He had *Scream* and *Scream 2* on DVD and wanted to watch them with someone who was into horror. CJ had apparently told him about my *Blair Witch* (www.blairwitch.com) obsession. I've watched it maybe thirty times total.

I was thinking that Nick probably missed CJ and figured I was the next best thing. It wasn't like I hadn't played this role before. Once in a while, Shay's guys come by and hang out with me when Shay isn't available. It's like they feel connected to Shay by being with me. I am their personal Jan Brady giving them the inside info on their oh-so-hot Marcia (I know I sound like I'm a freak about *The Brady Bunch*). They always tried to get me to spill some inside info on her too. As if I'd bother trying to tell them the truth about Shay. Whipped guys are totally deaf and blind, in my opinion.

It was no big deal, but Nick isn't older like Shay's men, so I felt a little weird. None of CJ's or Tasha's guys had come to my house before; they usually cried on my shoulder at school. First I stashed the bowl of Doritos and M&M's in the pantry for later, and then I started picking up the slobbed-out living room. This involved stuffing stacks of worn-out *Cosmopolitan*s and *Lucky*s into the closet, rubbing a paper towel over the dust-crusted coffee table, and kicking my mom's half-dozen shoes into the hall closet. I even sprayed a little Lysol. My mom and Shay sometimes smoke to stay skinny.

The décor in our living room and kitchen is really casual. We don't have much furniture, and none of it really matches. No one cleans much or picks up much either. My sister and mom sink all their capital into themselves. In Angela's and Shay's minds, their beautiful faces and bods are much better investments than house stuff. I'm not saying our house is bad or anything. It's just your average middle-class ranch (that's the way the rental lady described it to us).

I wasn't about to do more in the living room. This was CJ's guy, after all. If he'd been mine, I might have gotten out the vacuum cleaner.

Next stop was the bathroom mirror. I looked kind of blah. Even if it were just Tasha or CJ coming over, I'd usually try to pull myself together. I tilted my head down and blasted the blow-dryer over my long, pin-straight hair, hoping for some pouf. My hair is semi-thick, so it worked. I splashed on some of my mom's sexy perfume and rubbed blush into my cheeks. I needed a lot more, of course. Like a barrel of mascara and yards of eye pencil. I don't do much with makeup, despite being practically raised on Clinique and Maybelline. I mean, it would be like trying to compete with Shay and Angela, which I'd never want to do.

I was running to the bedroom to change clothes when it hit me again that Nick was just a guy, not a guy-guy (the latter being someone you want to hook up with). He didn't count. He wasn't a prospective boyfriend or a prospective anything. I hadn't had a date in ages and was obviously turning into a spaz.

Nick was almost like a girl. Really.

Not.

MESSAGE BOARD

✉ NICK IS HOT. I DON'T BLAME HER— 007U90—AT 11:13 P.M.

Nick Pilates is sooooo hot, guys ☺ ☺. I don't blame genesis for wanting to hang with him. god, I've never had the nerve to talk to him. Some people say he's a player, but like I said, I don't listen to rumors. Anyway, Genesis was just being like a friend. Nothing wrong with watching scary movies with a friend. I like comedy and romance better though.

✉ **Re: NICK IS HOT, I DON'T BLAME HER— queenSheba—at 12:35 a.m.**

i just can't agree, 007ugo. i mean about genesis watching movies with nick, NOT about nick being hot, because he is so cute. (i don't believe he's a player either.) i wouldn't like my best friend to watch movies alone with my guy. i'm not saying genesis asked for trouble, but it makes you wonder.

✉ **Re: NICK IS HOT, I DON'T BLAME HER— 007ugo—at 12:45 a.m.**

You've got to give her a chance, queenSheba. being judgmental sucks. doesn't everyone agree?

✉ **Re: NICK IS HOT, I DON'T BLAME HER— JUICYFRUIT45—at 6:34 a.m.**

i hate people judging me! but I might get jealous if my girlfriend spent time alone with my guy. Arghh! I don't know what to think!

CONFESSIONS OF A BOYFRIEND STEALER— BLOG BY GENESIS BELL

[3RD ENTRY]

Wait till you hear how it all went down between Nick and me, okay? Then you can judge all you want.

← →

So, the doorbell rang, and Nick Pilates was standing there in the flesh.

He was all slouchy, and his hair was kind of messed up. He looked kind of like a cross between a preppy boy and a derelict.

He said, "Hey, Gen."

I, being a brilliant wit, said, "Hey back."

We stared at each other until Nick said, "Can I come in?"

I gawked like a geek but finally opened the door, letting Nick and a blast of fresh cool air in.

We both kind of slumped our way to the couch. Nick was carrying a pizza and a liter of Coke.

"Dinner," he said. "If you're nice, I'll let you eat the mushrooms." He grinned.

"Mushrooms are barf," I said.

"Then you're out of luck."

"Ha. What a hero." I went to the kitchen and snagged a new bag of Oreos. "I may share these with you if you're nice. Consider them my dinner and your dessert."

"You got Hershey's syrup? These are better when you can dunk 'em."

I made a face. I didn't really know if we had syrup or not, but c'mon. His cookie combo idea was gross.

"So, what's up with CJ?" He munched a slice, managing not to make a huge mess. "She IMs me the shortest, most boring crap ever." He propped his feet up on the coffee table.

He opened the Coke bottle and poured us each some in the mugs I had just set out. I plunked down beside him on the couch.

"I can't believe she took off for Cancún and left me here. I thought we were going to have this awesome break together."

I tried to drink slowly, to avoid the big-gulp burp effect. "What were you guys going to do?"

"I don't know," Nick griped. "Something. All I know is that everyone is gone. They're all partying and drinking their asses off either on the beach or in the mountains."

"Except for you and me," I pointed out.

"Yeah, my dad's making me work at his green-house. This whole vacation sucks."

"CJ will be back soon," I said. "Then you'll feel better."

"I just hope she's not going crazy down there. It's not like she's the nun type, you know."

No duh. But did that mean they had like an open relationship? CJ was so casual about Nick in many ways. Did Nick *expect* her to be unfaithful? Hard to fathom. Despite being a free agent type, CJ seemed to really dig Nick. At least, I thought she did.

We drank our Cokes in silent unison. I glanced at Nick and noticed again that even scruffy he was a nice piece of eye candy. CJ was lucky, but then CJ always was. I can't remember her without a love-struck guy at her heels. Even way back in junior high. CJ has always had that something extra, besides ultralong legs, a per-fectly flat stomach, and a cover-girl face. Her only downfall is baby-fine, thin hair. But who notices? Be-sides catty, jealous girls.

To break the sudden silence, I pointed to the DVD on the table. "You brought *Scary Movie 2*."

"I know." He got up and shoved it into the player. "I couldn't find the *Scream*s." He shrugged. "My brother probably took them. Anyway, this one's good for a few laughs."

"I love that one scene when that chick flies through the air." I snickered. "It's stupid but definitely funny. My cousin Alison from Texas says the movie's better when you're high."

Immediately, I wanted to kick myself. What a dumb thing to say. I was the straightest person around. I hate it when I try to sound cool and sound stupid instead.

"Why, you got a doobie or something?" Nick looked only mildly interested.

"No, I don't smoke," I said. In my fantasies, I've tried everything and anything. In reality, I'm a total chicken.

Nick stared at me for a second. A vaguely surprised expression lit up his blue eyes. Either that or a piece of pizza cheese was stuck in his teeth.

"You're okay, Gen." He poured us some more Coke. "Too many people put on these big fronts, you know? Always trying to be what they're not."

I didn't know what to say. I was one of those people most of the time, at least on the inside. Always wishing I was better or more exciting than I really was. I drank my Coke too quickly and had to swallow a burp. Aware that Nick was still staring at me, I decided I had to say something.

"Guess what, I'm going to make a documentary about Fiesta Beach."

"You're kidding? Like a real show for TV?" He seemed interested.

"Well, it'll be for school cable at first, but maybe MTV will want to air it." Was that my mouth moving on its own? I swear I hadn't thought about what would happen after I made the show. My mouth had a mind of its own.

"That would be awesome, Gen," Nick said. He grinned at me. "So, can I be the star?" He flexed and posed. "I'm the best bartender around, which I know you know because you've seen my work. You gotta admit I make killer cocktails, and everyone loves my Nick Pilates Vodka Specials."

"You'll be in it, I promise, and maybe you'll even be a main character. But the party itself is the show centerpiece." Again my mouth was just blabbing away all on its own. At least it was saying stuff that was kind of smart.

Because really, I did have to look at the big picture. Maybe I wouldn't make the Terribles the exclusive focus after all. Maybe I'd pick a broader cast of characters—I could include Nick and as many hot guys as I could find. Hey, it works for the WB.

Nick snickered. "Wait till CJ hears that. I bet she thinks you'll change it to the CJ Thompson show."

I snickered too. "I know, I know. Anyway, I want this documentary to be amazing. I want it to capture the whole Fiesta Beach atmosphere."

"I bet MTV will buy it, Gen. It's gotta be better than the crap they're showing these days."

I never realized Nick could be so sweet.

"So, tell me the truth? Is CJ screwing around down there or what?"

I squinted, wondering how to answer. By screwing around, did he mean sleeping with other guys? Then the answer was I don't know and probably. If he meant flirting and hooking up, then the answer was a big fat yes.

I was silent too long.

"That's okay," Nick said. "You don't have to tell me."

He ran his hands through his hair just then, which made him look even scruffier and cuter.

"It's not like you guys are married, right?" I laughed a little. I was cool. But then I remembered I should be protecting CJ's interests. "Anyway, CJ likes you a lot, and that's all that matters, right?"

Nick yawned and pushed his hair the other way. He leaned back, looking very much at home.

"Yeah, you're right," he agreed. "CJ's my goil. We got a thing, and ain't nothin' gonna come between us."

I think he was trying to do a New Jersey *Sopranos* accent. It wasn't bad, but it wasn't great.

"You're not gonna do that accent on my show, are you?" I grinned at him.

"Hey, show some respect," he said back, still trying to sound all *Sopranos.*

It made me laugh, but I didn't want him to think I was bitchy. "Don't worry, you can say whatever you want."

He fake-punched my arm. "Just so you know who's boss." Still doing that horrible Mafia voice.

"Ha, ha." I made a face. Something made me say, "So, is that why you came over? To try out your accent on me?"

"Ha, ha. Right. I just thought you'd be fun to hang out with." He gave me an innocent puppy-dog look, so I didn't mention that I thought he was just after info on CJ.

He hit the Play button on the remote.

I leaned back and tried to relax. It was just good old Nick and good old Genesis, two buds. Down for some movie time. I had Oreos, *Scary Movie* 1 and 2, and safe, nonromantic male companionship. Why shouldn't I enjoy myself?

Four hours later, Nick and I were practically bug-eyed. All the Coke, the Oreos, and the pizza were gone. Nick was lying on the sofa with his legs in my lap. But it was companionable, not sexual. Okay, now, Shay's guys had never gotten that close, but sometimes they'd sit right next to me. So this really wasn't that different. And Nick was a friend of a friend, so it was okay.

Sure his legs felt warm and solid and cozy. Sure it felt good being close, but not dangerous in any way. Even when Nick played with my hair, it was just friendly. I remember Shay's guy Justin did that once. And it was cool.

I liked when Nick did it, but in a platonic way. Okay, when his fingertips brushed my collarbone by accident I did get the chills for a second, but I was way too tired and too full to feel even a drop of real erotic excitement. It was all just very friendly.

Message Board

✉ **So, what is Fiesta Beach really?**—
juicyfruit45—at 9:45 a.m.
Just curious. I've heard it gets really wild, but I don't know anyone who's gone. I think genesis and nick weren't doing anything wrong, not that much. maybe they should have sat on separate chairs or something? just to be safe?

✉ **Re: So, what is Fiesta Beach really?**—
queensheba—at 3:11 p.m.
i've never been to fiesta beach, but it is really huge here in jamaica plains. it's supposed to be the best party ever. i can see why genesis wanted to film it. i can't wait till i go next year!! i think genesis should have sent nick home. i feel sorry for cj.

✉ **Re: So, what is Fiesta Beach really?**—
007ugo—at 2:37 a.m.
Omigod! CJ is terrible to her boyfriends! She is so unfaithful and always has been! Everyone knows it. She has to make every single guy on the planet fall in love with her. I can't wait to see the fiesta Beach documentary. I didn't go this year. I've never gone (big parties aren't my scene).

✉ **Re: So, what is Fiesta Beach really?**—
juicyfruit45—at 11:22 a.m.
I can't really talk about CJ since I don't know her at all.

✉ Re: So, what is Fiesta Beach really?—
QueenSheba—at 11:56 a.m.

007ugo, i think it's wrong to dog cj, even if you don't like her. you can't blame her for what genesis and nick did.

MOST RECENT ENTRIES   CALENDAR

VIEW FRIENDS   LINKS   PHOTOS

`02/04 07:14:59`

Confessions of a Boyfriend Stealer—
Blog by Genesis Bell

[4TH ENTRY]

No one should ever feel sorry for CJ, trust me. As for Nick and me, well, we didn't *plan* any of it. . . . Stuff just happens, you know? You'll see.

← →

When Nick staggered to his feet and announced he was splitting, I had no thought whatsoever of kissing him. I swear it. I was feeling relaxed and mellow. The night had gone on so long that it felt as if Nick and I were the last two survivors of a disaster.

You know how it is when time is a blur, and you kind of don't feel like yourself, and everything is all dreamy and abnormal. Sometimes that weird kind of intimacy can be a good thing, though. I remember once when my mom and my sister and I spent the night in the basement waiting out a tornado. The three of us huddled tight and told gross-out stories to pass the time. It's one of my best family memories.

As I followed Nick to the door, all I kept thinking about was that it was late and I was going to crash as soon as Nick left. I also hoped my mom wouldn't be dragging some new boyfriend in that night. You can OD on all of that cute sex stuff. Giggles, innuendos, neck nuzzling, leg grabbing, the whole number. Barf.

Nick paused at the door. I was straining to hear if a car had pulled up. I was hoping against hope that my mom and her new love victim wouldn't show up. Seeing them would kill my pleasantly spacey mood.

"Hey, Gen," Nick said, yawning. "Leaden is playing at the Blue Circle tomorrow. They try too hard to be street, and they're way too heavy on the bass, but it could be a laugh. Want to come and split a pitcher?"

He yawned again. He had very nice teeth.

I gawked at him. The Blue Circle is a crappy dive in a crappy neighborhood. But they aren't exactly legal, and if you have money, they serve you, no questions asked. I'd heard people talking about it, and I knew in a while it was going to be *the* cool place to go. I knew CJ and Tasha hadn't been there yet. I'd be the first one to experience the Blue Circle. Man.

"Sure, why not?" I nonchalantly flipped my hair back.

We were friends, right? If one of Shay's guys asked me, I'd say yes, right? None of CJ's or Tasha's guys had asked me to a concert before, but so what? If Chi asked, I'd say yes too.

I swear I didn't plan what happened next. I kind of looked up at Nick. I was standing a little close, but we weren't toe to toe. I maybe, really just maybe, might have licked my lips a little. But hey, it was winter, and they were dry. So what, anyway? It's not like I'm your average sex kitten.

Nick put his hands on my shoulders, and I thought he was going to say something buddy-buddy like "See ya later" or "It's been fun," but then he kissed me.

I was so surprised that I lost my balance, but Nick grabbed me and held on to me. Our bodies were totally touching. Having Nick kiss me was a huge shock, but a good one. Kind of like biting into a chocolate and finding out it's filled with really rich, really delicious mousse. Yum. I couldn't catch my breath, and the ground seemed to shift under my feet.

Nick's kiss was perfect, firm but gentle. His lips were nice and hot and soft. His kiss was giving me the shivers; I didn't even think of stopping anything. He smelled like fabric softener and cologne. His body was warm and hard and nice, because he's really into weight training and running. As you can tell, I noticed a lot during that one kiss, which wasn't quite long enough.

Nick and I stepped back and grinned at each other like a couple of stoners who had just given in to a bad case of the munchies.

I was thinking that I was really glad Shay had given me a lecture a few years before on how to be a good kisser. It isn't that hard to remember. There are three don'ts: don't slobber, don't keep your lips clenched together, *but* don't drill your tongue into a guy's mouth. The do part is simple: act like you enjoy it, and if you do put your tongue in his mouth, be delicate. Moaning and running your hands through the guy's hair are optional.

I think I did some of the dos, and I prayed I didn't do any of the don'ts. If you want to learn more about kissing, I suggest you go to www.virtualkiss.com.

The New Year's before, one of Shay's guys had kissed me really quick on the lips; the year before that this drunken sophomore at a party tried to eat my face but I was able to push him away before I actually hurled. Before Nick, that was my sad experience with kissing.

You gotta understand that I'd gone out with maybe three guys in my entire life and the last time was to the coin laundry. Yeah, this jerk actually asked me out last year to do his laundry. That's a perfect example of what my so-called love life used to consist of. I really was a late bloomer, just like CJ and Tash said.

Before I could even consider a second kiss, a car door slammed shut.

"Crap," I whispered. Talk about being doused in ice water.

Nick raised an eyebrow. He seemed remarkably unruffled. My heart was galloping in my chest, and I was suddenly sweating like crazy. Luckily, he hadn't tried to touch my underarms or anything. Not that any guy would.

"It's my mother."

Of course, Angela Bell wouldn't care if she caught me making out with a guy—even if he was my friend's guy. Did you really think she would? The problem was not that at all. I should have been relieved that she was stopping me from kissing my best friend's boyfriend a second time, but I wasn't. One more kiss wouldn't have hurt. I mean, I only got one chocolate. How fair was that? My lips were so ready for more kisses. It's not like it was sex, which is superbig cheating instead of minor cheating.

At least Nick was with me instead of some hot mama ho bag. At least I wouldn't let things get out of hand and there was no worry he'd catch anything gross, since I've been so pathetically pure all my life.

I made a face. "She's probably bringing home some new boyfriend."

"So?"

I sighed. It was tough to explain. I tried. "Picture your mom or your dad."

He nodded.

"Now picture them making out with some stranger. I mean really making out, with kissy-face and groping and everything."

Nick grimaced. "That's gross, Gen."

I nodded and reached up to touch my lips. They were still tingling, but they were cooling off. Sadly.

My mom came banging through the door just then, wearing the sappiest smile imaginable. But surprise, surprise, she was solo.

"Hey, y'all," she said, sashaying right by us. She plopped onto the couch and propped her feet on the coffee table. "Lord, I am in another world, Genesis. Wait till I tell you." She stretched her arms over her head, still wearing that bizarre smile. I don't think she really saw Nick or me. "I'm just walking in the clouds right about now."

Nick gaped at her. My mother is a cross between Pamela Anderson and Kathie Lee Gifford. I admit that's an unusual combo. Extreme Barbie meets prissy talk-show host, but my mom carries it off. Despite the boob job and BOTOX injections, though, Angela is a little rough around the edges. The fact that she was in a Lycra mini and high heels made her even more impossible to ignore. Nick couldn't drag his eyes away, but I'm used to it. Why bother getting jealous over a fact that will never change?

Also, my mother is not from the South, though she's picked up some mannerisms from her Southern men friends. People are always disoriented by her accent contrasting with Shay's and my bland non-Southern twang.

"Mom," I said, "this is Nick—" I was about to add that he was CJ's boyfriend, just to be honest, you know, but she cut me off.

"Nice to meet ya." She lit a cigarette. "I should give these up. They make you crinkle like an old prune. Genesis knows I'd never let her smoke." She closed her eyes and inhaled deeply.

She didn't open her eyes. Nick and I exchanged furtive glances and walked back to the door.

Nick shuffled his feet. I thought he was going to retract his invitation to the Blue Circle, but he tweaked my nose and said, "Pick ya up at eight." He was really cool about it. So obviously one little kiss wasn't a big deal.

I nodded like a dummy as the door shut behind him.

"CJ and Nick are crazy about each other," I announced, knowing my mother wasn't paying any attention.

I rubbed my lips. They felt weird to the touch. I picked up my shoes and tossed a pillow back onto the sofa.

Was it really that big a deal? So what if our mouths touched? We were just being friendly. I heard that in Europe everyone kisses everyone. CJ always says she'd rather be a European because they're more sophisticated. She'd understand. I'm sure she would. If she ever found out, which I was sure she never would.

My head started to hurt. Thinking was irritating me.

"Genesis . . . I just have to tell ya, honey. I'm in love!" my mom announced just as I was about to head for the Tylenol in the bathroom. She was gazing at the ceiling now. She sucked hard on her cigarette. I was amazed she remembered I was in the room.

I stopped touching my mouth. Her words had just sunk in. "What?"

"I met the most wonderful man. I think he's the One."

"Did you say you're *in love*?"

For years, I've watched my mom wade through an endless sea of adoring men, and I've never, ever heard her use those words. At best, she was "fond of" or "really into" the guy of the moment.

Angela Bell in love? For some reason, that sent shivers up my spine.

"Look what he gave me," she said, holding out her wrist. She was wearing a bracelet. It wasn't real gold or silver (I can tell by now, having seen tons of jewelry my mom's received over the years), and it didn't have diamonds on it.

"W-W-J-D," I read aloud. What would Jesus do. . . . I don't know. Run for the hills. Let hell freeze over. Turn wine into water.

"Kenny is so sweet. And very moral." My mom giggled in a creepy, never-before-heard way. "He's a churchgoing man."

"You mean kind of like that televangelist with the big hair and sideburns?"

My mother glared at me. "Absolutely not. He's really religious, not some phony oddball."

I shrugged. We'd never even mentioned religion in the Bell household before.

"He doesn't believe in premarital sex, in—in most cases." Her tone was reverent.

I didn't know what to say. This was way too *Twilight Zone.*

"As soon as Kenny gets his divorce, he wants to talk about us getting serious. Maybe even going ring shopping." My mom sighed dreamily. "Kenny's family has a lot of real estate, you know. But he likes to live simple. He's not one to flash it around."

I was sure Angela would change that if she was around long enough. I was glad to know that my mom hadn't totally lost it; I would have fainted if she'd told me Kenny was some guy with an average working-class income.

"How long have you known this guy?" Not that it mattered. My mom has gotten proposals after knowing guys for a day.

"Two weeks. I didn't want to talk about it right away and ruin the magic."

"That's nice, Mom," I said. I wanted to ask, Are you on drugs? But I restrained myself. First, she would have laughed at me. Second, I didn't really want to get into the whole craziness that is my mom's love life.

I really just wanted to escape to my room.

My mom called out, "Gen, hon, did you pay the Saks bill? I need to get a new outfit for Kenny."

I yelled back "Yes!" and shut the door to my bedroom. My life was getting exciting. I had Nick's kisses and my Fiesta Beach documentary to think about. But honestly, I only really wanted to think about the kissing. I wanted to think about why I wasn't feeling all that guilty for kissing CJ's boyfriend. I thought if I analyzed it enough, I would see it was no big deal. I was a Jan Brady Terrible. No one on this planet would worry about Nick and me going to see Leaden together.

So why should I?

I checked my Palm Pilot and my PC. No e-mails from CJ. I knew she was out partying and flirting and maybe even hooking up.

She was a twenty-first-century kind of girl. Why shouldn't I be one too?

I flopped on my bed, which is a reject of Shay's. It's perfectly round with a pink spread. I think it's cool and retro. Shay said it was too juvenile. The bamboo miniblinds with the painted tigers on them were Shay's too. They're too cheesy for her now. The Tweety clock was a gift from one of Angela's boyfriends, who was a big fan of cartoons. The only Genesis part of the room is my stuffed-animal collection, which happens to be all dogs. The Akita and poodle are my favorites. They're a reminder that I'll be able to get real pets once I move out on my own someday. (Angela and Shay are allergic to everything furry—right!) I grabbed the Akita and hugged him hard. The other cool part of my room is my photo collection, which I have hanging above my PC, and which I also love. Most of the pictures are of CJ and Tasha, but I have one old one of my father, just to remind me that I'm not *only* related to Angela and Shay. Don't worry; I'm not the sappy type. I mean, I hardly know the guy.

I avoided looking at CJ's picture as I flipped over onto my stomach and closed my eyes. It was deep dark, but then I saw weird splashes of colors and lights. They were spinning and making me dizzy. Even when I opened my eyes I saw multicolored designs in the air. I was having my own mini freak-out trip without the drugs. I sat up and grabbed my Palm Pilot.

Tasha. That was who I needed to contact. Okay, she never answered IMs or e-mails while she was skiing, but I'd do it anyway.

Hey, u thr? I typed on my Palm Pilot. *It's Gen.* I waited and was about to turn it off when a message popped up.

I couldn't believe it. Maybe I really was high and didn't know it. Maybe Nick had laced the pizza with PCP.

Cool here ☺. *met a gr8 guy. hot kisser* ☺ *details l8er . . . tash*

I had to IM back. ☺ *but chi?*

She flashed back quickly. *Not married! TTYS. tash.*

I tossed my Palm Pilot onto my desk and stretched out on the bed. Tasha was right. We were all single, so what was the big deal? Messing around and flirting were all part of the game. Tash was cheating on Chi, as usual.

At least Nick wasn't cheating on CJ, because as long as he was with me, he was safe. I know CJ would hate it if he were with some slut stranger.

Really, when you think about it, I was just boyfriend-sitting.

I decided to consider what I would wear to the Leaden concert. Something sophisticated but subtle.

Relaxed and laid-back but sexy. Sexy in a friendly, not-too-serious way but also in a way that would definitely make Nick notice. That kind of outfit sounded complicated and not remotely like anything I owned. Which meant it was time to raid Shay's closet.

I got up and glanced at my Palm Pilot. I had a message.

Thx for the Oreos. xxx nick

I grinned and typed back. *Thx for the pizza. ooo gen*

I had to be polite, right? Even though I didn't eat any of the pizza. So you can see how friendly it all was. In our crowd, signing with Xs and Os was no big deal. It was all pretty low-key and casual.

Except for that one incredibly hot kiss, we were just buds.

Message Board

✉ JUST WRONG—QUEENSHEBA—AT 7:42 P.M.
see, guys, you can't make any more excuses! genesis KISSED nick, who was CJ'S boyfriend. that was just wrong!!! WRONG!!!!! i don't care what anyone says.

✉ Re: JUST WRONG—JUICYFRUIT45—AT 11:06 P.M.
I don't know. I think she and Nick just got carried away. I don't think anyone was really to blame. Anyway, it sounded like a really good kiss to me ☺. I have to admit, guys, I've been with some really, really bad

kissers so I'm kind of jealous of genesis's awesome experience (though I really do know, queenSheba, that it was wrong).

✉ Re: Just wrong—007ugo—at 1:23 a.m.

Okay, okay. Genesis made a bad judgment call, but it's not like she and Nick went too far. If they'd gone like to third base or something, that would have been sleazy.

Most Recent Entries   Calendar
View Friends   Links   Photos

03/04 02:12:01

Confessions of a Boyfriend Stealer—
Blog by Genesis Bell

[5th Entry]

I knew some of you would totally misunderstand. But like 007ugo said, Nick and I did *not* go overboard. We never even got near *second* base (let alone third)! We just kissed, and I'd never done anything like it before. Never. Ever. So you can see I wasn't exactly prepared for what happened.

← →

The next morning, I woke up from a bizarre dream that involved me skiing in my underwear and ballet slippers. No skis, just slippers. And I was blindfolded. I definitely didn't want to examine the Freudian implications. You know, blindly heading for disaster and that kind of stuff.

The first thing I heard was Shay's voice booming down the hallway. Shay is petite and adorable but has a big, deep voice that would be better suited to a tattooed muscleman in a leather bar. My first thought was that she was pissed that I'd taken her low riders and brand-new black sweater.

Then I heard her more clearly.

"Mother, *how* can you date a born-again? You know how I feel about them. I have a phobia about those people. . . ."

I couldn't believe how quickly they had gotten onto the subject of my mother's new boyfriend. Shay must have just gotten in. It usually would have taken them hours to catch up, since she'd been gone a week. Typically they'd be exchanging stories about how many men had come on to them and how many women had tried to pick fights with them. You know, that sort of stuff. Those two were the proverbial peas in a pod. Usually.

"Kenny is different. Wait till you meet him. He's sexy and really more spiritual than religious. . . ."

"Are you taking those diet pills again?" Shay's voice was a mix of scorn and fear.

My stomach heaved, and I tucked my head under the pillow. I so didn't want to deal with my family today, but from time to time I have to keep an eye on them. If I didn't, God knows what could happen.

I wanted to focus on Nick.

"I'm in love, silly. For the first time." My mother practically sang this out. "You of all people, Shay, should be happy for me."

There was no reply to that absurd statement. Instead, footsteps stomped down the hall and my door was flung open.

"I suppose you've heard about this Jesus freak of Mom's," Shay said, sitting down heavily on my bed. "She says she's in love with him! She's never in love with anyone. She's such a liar." Shay didn't bother with "Hello" or "Good morning" or "How was your week?" She had a bottle of water in one hand and a bottle of vitamin E in the other. Angela had told her to take lots of E to fight the effects of working in a smoke-filled bar and of smoking the "occasional" cigarette.

"I think she's lost it. God, I'm gone for one week and that woman totally goes crazy."

I sighed and pulled the pillow from my head. I stared at my scowling sister and tried to feel a little sympathy. You see, Shay and my mother are usually so tight that they really are like twins. Think Mary-Kate and Ashley. Now Angela was suddenly doing her own thing, and Shay was left out in the cold. No wonder she was freaking out.

"Mom told me about Kenny last night," I said. "But they hardly know each other."

Shay flipped her hair back. She looked gorgeous and tanned. "Maybe it's hormones, because usually Mom is so cool about men. She's acting gross now."

I sat up. I guessed I'd better calm her down. "Look, it's probably just a phase. You know how she is. Remember when she was into bodybuilders, and then it was old grandpa types. . . ."

"Maybe you're right," Shay said, looking mollified. "But this love stuff? How could she do this to me?"

"Even if Angela just *thinks* she's in love, we should be cool, right? This is important stuff for her, and she'll get pissed if we give her a hard time." Sure, it was creepy as hell, and maybe it was just puppy love, but still, everyone knows you've got to take any kind of love seriously.

"She's not in love," Shay said. Her bottom lip was jutting out.

I stared at Shay and tried to decide if I really wanted to get into this with her. Yeah, right. She and Angela would work it out. They always did.

"Give it a rest, okay? It's just a phase, like I said."

"If you say so." She stared at the ceiling and then looked back at me. "Hey, I think the shower needs to be fixed. The water's not coming out right."

I sighed. "The plumber says there's nothing he can do unless we want a new shower installed. The landlord said no way."

Shay made a face and headed for the door. Shay and Angela were totally oblivious about what was going on with me. I was pretty hyped about Nick, but my sister and my mom didn't have a clue. No surprise, really.

I looked at my Tweety clock. Half past ten. Almost ten hours till my date—okay, my *meeting* with Nick. Timing is everything, I reminded myself.

"Do you care if I wear your new sweater and black suede pants?" I shot out as quickly and nonchalantly as possible.

"Whatever," Shay said, slamming the door behind her.

Cool. I grinned. My mother's love life was working in my favor for once.

Listen, I'm not a mean person, though maybe you think so because I didn't get all upset over Shay and Angela's latest drama. I was just so used to those two. I could have even been like them (God forbid). I mean, I had the chance.

When I was about six, Angela and my sister were really into beauty pageants, especially the mother-daughter ones. They mostly did local stuff, though I remember being dragged out of state once or twice. They made sure to enter shows that focused on "presentation," since neither of them had any beauty-queen-type talents, like singing, dancing, magic, or ventriloquism, to show off.

Well, some ditzy pageant consultant friend of my mother's swore that having me join in would give them more winning power. She claimed a beautiful mom with two beautiful daughters would just melt the judges' hearts.

My mother pleaded, begged, and bribed me into finally having my hair permed, since it was decided that I definitely needed some beautifying. Angela swore she'd think about letting me have a puppy if I'd wear a dress and makeup and prance around onstage with her and Shay while some dork in a suit sang something really corny, like "Pretty Woman" or "Isn't She Lovely."

So she bought a home perm kit, and there I was in the kitchen with my hair half permed when the smell suddenly made me want to puke. I just couldn't stand it. Even the thought of a puppy didn't help. I just remember my eyes watering and my stomach heaving. With my mother screaming at me to stop and come back right this second, I raced into the bathroom and jumped into the shower with all my clothes on. I refused to let her finish. Besides, those pageants were creepy—too much canned, staticky music, killer perfume, and women overdoing the makeup. Some of the contestants were as scary as circus clowns (who truly freak me out). I'd much rather have been next door at Mrs. Jewel's house. She babysat me while Angela and Shay were at the pageants. Mrs. Jewel was chubby and good-natured and wore housecoats most of the time (Angela thought she was a disaster), but she let me play with the family cocker spaniel and watch *Bewitched* and *I Dream of Jeannie* and tons of other old shows. I loved staying with Mrs. Jewel.

Angela was furious over my perm disaster. Shay laughed her ass off; she didn't really want me onstage with them anyway.

For a while, I had a very weird hairdo—half curly, half pin-straight. I was banned from the beauty pageant life, which Angela and Shay quit a year later anyway. Angela said ugly, jealous women ran the pageants and it was all a huge waste of her time.

After that, Angela realized I wasn't a part of the

Angela-Shay club, so she lets me do my own thing (though that doesn't stop her or Shay from giving me tips on beauty and men from time to time). They mainly count on me to take care of bills and repairs and stuff like that.

So give me a break, okay? We have a system, and it mostly works.

By the time I was showered and dressed, my mom and sister were both out of the house. I guessed Shay had rushed over to Justin's house for comfort (Justin is her standby guy), while my mom was probably at Kenny's, or maybe she was shopping. For all I knew she was in church.

I had made up my mind. The kiss between Nick and me was great. Sensational, if I was being really honest. But really, I was going to the concert with him to keep an eye on him. You know—boyfriend-sitting? It was my duty to go to the Blue Circle that night.

As I hot-rolled my hair, I reminded myself that Nick and I just got a little bored and a little carried away the night before. We were just good buds on some major sugar rush after scarfing down all those Oreos and guzzling all that Coke.

I was careful with my makeup. "Always use upward motions when applying foundation," my mom had instructed me when I was ten, "and you'll prevent sags and wrinkles down the road. You'll thank me someday, Genesis. Too many girls just don't know how to apply blush right. You'll be way ahead of the game."

For Angela, that was what was called a motherly moment.

I stared in the mirror and practiced a sophisticated smile. Not bad. Actually, I looked really good, as conceited as that sounds. Despite that, Nick and I were definitely going to be cool that night. The kiss would be a juicy little secret, but that was it. If Nick made a move, I'd be casual and play it off. I'd be a good boyfriend-sitter.

I sighed and went downstairs to make myself lunch. Jalapeño cream cheese on banana bread. I'd be good that night, I promised myself.

← →

By the time it was eight o'clock and I was ready for Nick to arrive, my mom was parked on the couch. She was smoking, as usual, but get this, she was actually knitting too. Or at least, she was trying to. She was clanking the needles around and she had yarn everywhere. I was curious to see if she'd ask me why I was dressed up and where I was going. She didn't. She just kept humming and clattering her needles, only pausing to chain-smoke her Virginia Slims.

Magazines were heaped on the floor. The coffee table was covered with dirty mugs, hair clips, lipsticks, and an empty bag of chips. A few cigarette butts had landed on the carpet.

Shay came into the living room and glared at her. She had a cell clasped to her ear and was snarling into it. "EJ, I mean it. If you want to see me tonight, you'd better get here like in ten minutes. . . . Tomorrow I have a double shift and—"

The doorbell rang. Shay stomped over to get it before I could even flinch. As soon as she spotted Nick, looking all Hollywood hottie, she went into automatic flirt mode. She smiled at him beguilingly and said, "Don't just stand there. Come on in." She'd never even met Nick, but that didn't stop her.

He couldn't resist giving her the once-over. No male, living or otherwise, could resist.

I waited for Shay to ask why Nick was here, but she didn't. He grinned at me, and my knees shook a little.

"It's just some friend of my sister's," I heard Shay say to an obviously jealous EJ. "She's in high school."

Just some friend. Yeah, that's what Nick was.

"You ready, Gen?" He patted his jacket. "We're gonna stay warm tonight, I promise." He showed me a flask tucked inside. I guessed it was Nick's homemade vodka. CJ was always making fun of how he was so proud of cooking up his own brew.

"See you guys," I said. "I'll probably be in late." Shay would have to have noticed by now that I'd done my hair and makeup, and even my nails. She'd have to be suspicious. I never went all out like this, ever. Not even for the few puny dates I've had in my life. But she just waved and walked off with the phone still glued to her ear, saying, "Listen, I want to go somewhere nice after work. Like the Golden Chalice. I need to relax with some good wine or I'll have a coronary. . . ."

My mom coughed on her cigarette and choked out, "Have fun." She smashed out her butt. "Just a sec," she said.

She dug into her purse and threw me a bottle of Visine. "Got to keep those eyes sparkly if you're going to be up all night." She winked playfully.

Angela knew her beauty dos, so I stuffed the Visine in my pants pocket.

"Thanks. Nick and I may be out all night," I said, giving it a shot.

At that exact moment, my mom put on headphones and started humming something that sounded a lot like "What a Friend We Have in Jesus." My sister was still whining into the cell. Everything was status quo.

I noticed that Nick was staring at Shay's ass as she disappeared into the kitchen. That too was typical. Men could no more resist my sister's ass than the average canine could resist a fresh, juicy T-bone.

Once inside Nick's car, I started to relax. It was chilly out, and I should have worn a jacket. I didn't realize I was uptight until I felt my neck muscles unkink. I have to say that Nick has a really nice ride. A black Corvette. I don't know cars, so I can't tell you the exact model, but it looked hot.

I couldn't picture me riding in it, even though that's exactly what I was doing. We made mindless small talk until Nick turned to me at a stoplight and said, "You know, you look great, Gen." He squinted.

"I mean it. I think you play it down, but you could give Tash and CJ a run for their money. You just don't put it out there like they do."

I shrugged modestly, but my heart gave a great big leap. Yeah, I admit it. I loved hearing that I looked hot. Hey, I even thought I looked pretty good. But I could feel my face turning bright red. Nick was staring at me for like several seconds.

"Uh, thanks" was my witty response.

I was relieved when we got to the Blue Circle, which looked as raunchy as I'd expected. Lots of bikes and jacked-up cars circled the unpaved lot, like they were ready to attack the building. Beer bottles and butts pretty much covered the pavement. A couple of people staggered out of the side door. They were dragging a comatose-looking guy behind them. He suddenly lurched out of their grip and started puking next to a Harley. I hoped it was his. His friends watched and cheered.

Nick and I just exchanged quick looks, like saying, Jerk can't hold his liquor. We passed a truck, which was bouncing a little, and we couldn't help seeing what was going on. Some girl was straddling a bearded man in the back. Why they weren't in the cab is beyond me. All in all, the Blue Circle was pretty crappy and pretty scary. In other words, perfect. Nick and I didn't touch as we headed for the door, but we walked close.

No one even bothered carding us when we walked in, though some tatted-up bald bouncer was getting high near the entrance. He looked rough. The second we stepped into the main room, we were sucked into this huge, squirming, noisy crowd wreathed in smoke. If you inhaled, you had to take in at least a quart of tar, nicotine, and marijuana. I'm sure the Blue Circle broke every code in the city book. Plus, most people were way older than us, like college age or older. I admit I was just a little freaked out.

I tried not to hang on to Nick, who didn't seem fazed by the scene at all. But then, guys can fake cool better than most girls.

A chick band was up on the stage. They were doing the heavy metal bit. All three had big eighties hair and gobs of eyeliner and blush. My mom would be horrified. Not one of them had properly blended. They were rocking out, though, and some people were moshing up near the front, while everyone else was drinking and talking. Some guy shouted to the band something like "Take your clothes off." They ignored him. A huge-breasted blonde flipped up her shirt, and everyone, including Nick and me, craned to take a look. (Fake, totally silicone, trust me).

The scene in the Blue Circle was just amazing, and suddenly, I could see myself producing a documentary here. I looked around and tried to picture where I'd set up cameras and lights. What if I filmed the piece from the bouncer's point of view? He was on the outside, but he was also an insider who knew everything that went on. Or I could do the show from a regular's viewpoint. Maybe the cameras could follow a waitress around. I must have been really staring, because Nick nudged me.

"What's up? You looking for someone?"

"I was just thinking, wouldn't it be cool to do like a documentary about the Blue Circle?"

"Yeah. Yeah, you're right." He squinted and scanned the room. "It could really work." He squinted some more and scratched his chin. "You'd definitely have to get some shots of the parking lot and maybe behind-the-scenes shots of the bands too." He was really into my idea, which was exciting. "It would be really cool, Gen. Too bad they'd never let you bring cameras in here."

"I know. It's just a fantasy." Cameras angling down from the ceiling would have been just too fantastic. I tried picturing how it would look from above with all the bodies jamming like crazy below. The smoke would give it such a funky look. A chill went up my spine. Maybe I *was* really cut out to be a big-time producer.

"I think you're going to make it big with this film business, Gen," Nick said, startling me.

"You do?" I could feel myself wanting to really grin but kept it down to a low-key smile.

"Yeah, you're smart and mature, especially compared to other kids."

I wanted to hear more, but I tried to look modest. "Uh, thanks."

"And you don't run your mouth like everyone else.

You listen." He narrowed his eyes thoughtfully. "I always get the feeling that you understand about life and stuff."

I'd have to check myself out in the mirror. Maybe I looked more worldly and sophisticated than I realized. And I was shocked that Nick could be so deep. Up until now, I'd always thought he was just boy fluff. You know, cute and fun, but not much more. Sort of like cotton candy. Cotton candy with awesome abs, that is.

Again I said, "Um, thanks." I know. Very sophisticated.

Nick pointed across the room. "Hey, look over there. An empty space near the wall. Let's go."

We moved fast. It was nice to finally have something to lean against, but the wall felt really sticky. I tried not to think of what it was doing to Shay's sweater.

I found myself staring at Nick, until he caught me and smiled. Embarrassed, I made myself watch the band.

It's not like it was bad that Nick and I were bonding some. We were friends, after all.

The chick band was winding down with their lead girl doing a long riff on the guitar. Her two sidekicks were bouncing and headbanging like crazy. They were amazing.

"Eye Candy," Nick said into my ear.

I squinted. The three of them looked rough to me. Not one of them had the body for the skimpy leather outfits they were wearing.

"Really? I thought you had better taste."

"No, dork. That's their name." Nick ruffled my hair. "They're not bad. Good vocals. Good guitar. They're probably better than Leaden."

"Then why are they just warm-up? Why isn't it the other way around?" Someone bumped me from behind and someone else elbowed me in the ribs. I tried to shift but I stepped on someone's foot. This scene was getting brutal. I had the urge to bite someone. Guess I was starting to fit in.

"Because they're chicks," Nick said. He held up a hand. "And before you go off on me, it's just the way the Blue Circle is. I didn't make the rules."

Someone hurled a pitcher of beer into the moshers, and a scuffle broke out. The tatted bouncer leaped into the middle of it and dragged a couple of scruffy-looking guys out.

Producing a show here would be kick ass. And I couldn't believe the nice things Nick had said about me, but I decided to think about them later. I wanted to have fun, not get serious.

I was dying of thirst and was thrilled when Nick pulled out his flask of home brew. My throat was already sore from the overload of smoke, and anything wet was appreciated. It wasn't as bad as CJ claimed it was. Maybe my taste buds were more refined than hers.

Leaden was starting up, and Nick was right: they weren't that great. But still, it was exciting to be part of the whole scene. It was so crowded that it was like we were all one collective sweaty flesh monster, shoulder to shoulder, mindlessly bouncing to Leaden's whacked-out tunes. Nick and I were close enough that I felt his warmth. We shared the flask, but neither of us went overboard. I wasn't into booze that much, and Nick whispered that he was going to be careful, since his older brother had lost his license for five years because of DUIs and that wasn't going to happen to him. The night flew by in a wildly pleasant, thunderous haze.

Right in the middle, I had to use the bathroom and made my way to the gross little nightmare that was labeled LADIES. I wished I had like a case of Lysol in there with me. The only good thing was that the lighting was dim so that I couldn't see just how disgusting it really was. But somehow it was inspirational, because while I was trying to squeeze soap out of the dispenser I got this idea for a show on the world's worst bathrooms; it would be the exact opposite of that one on the Travel Channel about the world's snazziest johns.

As I struggled through the crowd, I suddenly saw this super-sleazy girl hanging all over Nick. Can you believe it? I was gone like five minutes. She was older, maybe twenty. Her boobs were hanging out of her tank top and her hair had about a yard of black roots showing. Gross.

Nick waved, grinning foolishly.

"Gen, this is Tiffany," he said. He squeezed my shoulder. "I was just telling Tiffany that maybe you were lost."

"I wasn't." I glared at Tiffany of the really bad roots. She glared back at me.

I wasn't going anywhere, obviously.

Tiffany tossed her way overbleached hair. "Maybe I'll see you in here another time, Nick—alone."

She then slutted her way back into the crowd.

Nick grinned at me again. "I don't even know her."

I just rolled my eyes.

"Really," he said. He could have been telling the truth. All I know is that CJ said he was a big flirt and she couldn't trust him, which was probably part of his appeal. She sometimes liked a challenge.

He squeezed my shoulder again. "So, everything's okay?"

I said, "Whatever."

See how lucky CJ was that I was keeping an eye on Nick? I mean, we know Nick has a big player streak in him, so think of the trouble he'd have gotten into if I hadn't been there. What if he'd hooked up with that slutbag?

A few minutes later, Leaden stumbled off the stage, and the lights were on. I have to tell you that some of those rough customers looked really bad in the harsh fluorescents. Talk about coyote ugly. Nick still looked hot. Lucky him. I was afraid to check myself out in my pocket mirror.

I was thinking, Okay, Genesis, just because Nick was complimenting you and just because you kissed once doesn't mean jack. Remember, you're the boyfriend-sitter, and you and Nick are getting to be good friends. And that is that. We hadn't even held hands all night. We hadn't even brushed legs. Tasha once told me that leg touching is the biggest clue that a guy digs you.

We staggered out into the night, and like everyone, tore out of the parking lot as quickly as possible. Any glamour the Blue Circle had held earlier was totally gone.

I was trying not to yawn too much, and my eyes felt like grit. All that smoke, and some of it was clove and pot. I pulled out Angela's Visine and squirted in a few drops and offered it to Nick, who shook his head. He yawned and blinked. We were both quiet, listening to some new emo on the radio. I was feeling a little let down, but I told myself it was for my own good. Nick wasn't into me in that way, so no big deal. It could never happen anyway. I was cool. . . . Crap. I was bummed, even though I tried to tell myself I wasn't. I closed my eyes and tried not to feel too sad with the emo.

Suddenly we were stopping. We were right smack in the middle of bumper-to-bumper traffic. Nick started grumbling and swearing and smacking his hand on the steering wheel. I remembered CJ complaining about his road rage.

"I hate this," he whined. "We're not moving an inch."

I turned up the radio. "Guess we should just sit back and enjoy the view." I pointed to the line of cars in front of us and the dark fields on either side of us. We were now at a dead stop.

"Right." He scowled out the window. "Nothing but farms and crap."

"Exactly. I think they use crap to fertilize their farms," I cracked. I couldn't resist. Disasters always cheer me up. A good trait for living in the Bell household.

He ruffled my hair. "You are such a smartass."

I ruffled his hair too. "Takes one to know one."

He tickled me, and I tickled him back, and it seemed perfectly natural for us to start kissing. Playful kissing, I reassured myself. And it was totally dark, and no one in the cars around us could see anything, I figured. But then as things started getting really passionate, I stopped talking to myself altogether.

All I know is that I must have progressed from learning-it-by-the-book-kissing to advanced quick-learner kissing, because Nick seemed really into me and my lips. He was a good teacher.

Nick was kissing the back of my neck, which was turning every bone in my body into water, when I suddenly realized Alanis Morrisette was shouting on the radio about "Mr. Duplicity." Old song, I know, but her fury about her boyfriend's betrayal jolted me just enough. "You Oughta Know" hardly ever gets airtime since it's so ancient. Why tonight? It had to be an omen.

I pulled back from Nick reluctantly. He was so damned cute and such a good kisser. Remember CJ, I told myself. CJ. Your friend. She may be cheating on Nick, and they may have an open relationship, and maybe it's not true love, but it's totally sleazy to make out with CJ's guy. You are so much better than this.

"I think we should just, you know, be cool," I said.

He shrugged and then reached to adjust my shirt, which was off my shoulder. He winked at me, and I was relieved he wasn't upset or hurt. Luckily, traffic started moving a second later. The ride home was quick then. I kept telling myself it was okay. I hadn't done anything hugely horrible. Not really. Kissing is only a minor offense. We'd barely even Frenched. . . . Man, I couldn't believe I'd made out with Nick. Twice.

But maybe it was all a dream. Maybe it hadn't really happened. Right. That only happens in the soaps.

Neither of us talked much. Nick was humming with the radio and tapping his fingers on the steering wheel while he drove.

When he pulled up in my driveway, he looked like he wanted to kiss me goodnight, but instead he just said, "See ya soon, Gen."

I nodded and jumped out of the car. Like what did that mean?

When I got in, I saw a note taped to my bedroom

door. Tasha had called. She was home. She had news. I yawned. The news was probably a new pair of boots, or Tasha deciding to have a Brazilian wax (because if CJ was going to do it, than Tasha would have to as well). CJ and Tasha had been too squeamish to try it so far, but maybe CJ had taken the plunge. I climbed into bed without washing my face. It was two a.m. I was exhausted, but I was virtuous. Pretty much so.

MESSAGE BOARD

✉ Re: JUST WRONG—QueenSheba—at 10:27 P.M.

people never learn, do they? gen said she went out with nick 'cause she would keep him safe from other girls and then she kissed him a SECOND time. that was sick. i really think genesis's family is messed up and that is why she did the wrong thing. i can't imagine having a mom like angela! my mom would have never ever let me go out to the blue circle in the first place!

✉ Re: JUST WRONG—JUICYFRUIT45—at 11:06 P.M.

I think it might be cool to have a mom like Angela. my mom is way too strict. But Genesis and Nick, they seemed to really click, and they both were into movies and Nick was into Gen's documentary. I thought maybe they were almost falling for each other. Did anyone else think so? And has anyone else gone to the Blue Circle?

✉ <u>Re: JUST WRONG</u>—007U9O—aT 2:33 P.M.
I would love to go to the Blue Circle sometime. I heard about Leaden, and they are supposed to rock. I do think there was something special between Nick and Gen. Not just physical either.

03/04 05:55:49

CONFESSIONS OF A BOYFRIEND STEALER—BLOG BY GENESIS BELL

[6TH ENTRY]

I gotta be honest; Nick and I were never serious. Things just got out of hand (though I liked Nick a lot). I never thought about our having any kind of future. Really, I was wishing we had never had a past! You can understand, right? I mean, CJ and I were best buds. So were Tasha and I. We three were the Terribles. I was in way, way over my head.

← →

 Tasha looked awesome, depressingly so. She never gets that totally burned, hagged-out look so many girls get when they're really into skiing. You know, all red-faced and crinkly, with peely lips. Tasha had a pinkish glow and golden highlights in her thick wavy hair. Her lips are model pouty and her skin is perfect. She piles on the sunscreen, and of course, she's naturally gorgeous, not to mention stacked. Her fingers were loaded down with rings, as usual. Some had real gems in them, courtesy of rich, adoring Chi. She likes waving her hands around when she talks because it shows off her rings.

Tasha and I were sipping iced mocha espressos in the food court in Jamaica Plains Mall, which was swarming with people. She'd been calling all morning and leaving tons of voice mails while I'd slept in till practically noon. She said she had something *big* to tell me but that it was a secret and she had to tell me in person.

"I called a bunch of times last night. Your mom didn't answer until midnight. She said you were at the movies or something. She wasn't sure." Tasha paused to suck on her straw. "So where were you?"

I had been expecting this question, but still my heart jumped, and my palms turned icy.

Did Tasha know something? Was she trying to trap me? I felt like one of those guys on *Cops* who's being chased down by helicopters and angry-looking police on foot. Like I was about to be handcuffed and thrown to the ground. Luckily, I had rehearsed my lie and was prepared. I opened my mouth, but Tasha jumped up.

"This doesn't have enough ice in it. I'll be right back," she said, not waiting to hear my answer. She grinned at me. "I know you're dying to know everything, but you'll have to wait." She giggled and rushed off to the Coffee Bean stand.

Watching Tash, I felt a little sad. I was remembering the good times the Terribles have had—how we skipped school and snuck over to the local college to ogle the football players practicing. How we strolled through Cartier and pretended we were related to the Hiltons (and that we might actually buy diamond bracelets). How we convinced the security guys at a big rap concert that we knew the lead singer and got backstage (for about ten seconds).

Just a few months before, we'd sat in this very mall drinking double-shot espressos and rating all the guys who walked by. Tasha and CJ were much tougher judges than I was. Giggling, we kept score on napkins and wrote little comments like "cute butt" or "great abs" or "excellent smile." What made it even more fun was that no one around us knew what we were doing, though we did get some stares. Then CJ wrote the letters HP (Hottie Patrol) on our hands and said we should get T-shirts with official HP logos on them. We spent time doodling designs, though we never did get the shirts.

Those were the days. Lots of them were great. I'd just been a Terrible without any complications. I felt the iced mocha espresso slosh in my stomach.

Tasha was back carrying her new drink.

"Guess who's been in town for two whole days!" Tasha nearly shouted before she even sat down, her eyes shining excitedly.

It was tough to focus on what Tash was saying

because I was too busy trying to make myself look calm and normal.

"... she's got this gross rash all over her face and her body. She looks like a mutant, and—"

Tasha's words were seeping in. "Wait a minute. Who's got a rash? Are you talking about *CJ*?"

"Omigod, she's so upset. She's been going to this specialist, and she wears this huge hat and glasses 'cause she's so freaked out that someone will see her." Tasha lowered her voice. "She looks sooo bad. I couldn't believe it when I saw her."

My brain was in a whirl. "How long has she been home?"

"It's a total secret, Gen. She doesn't want anyone to know, especially Nick. She thinks he'll drop her if he sees her looking really ugly." Tasha leaned forward. "I only found out by accident. I was dropping off those sunglasses she loaned me, and I saw her peeking down the stairs while I talked with her mom." Tasha paused for breath. "Plus, she thinks the rash makes her look fat."

Despite my traumatized state, I made a face at the absurdity of that statement, even though it was typical CJ.

"I can't believe she didn't call me or, uh, Nick." I felt so guilty. While CJ had been scratching her rash, Nick and I had been kissing. Not just one time but twice.

"I don't blame her for hiding out. You wouldn't

either if you saw her. Anyway, she swore me to secrecy."

I was still trying to take it all in. "That is horrible. Poor CJ."

Tasha lowered her eyes, and her face sank a little. "Yeah, I know. I really feel for her. You know that."

CJ hiding out for two days, not talking to anyone, not seeing anyone. This was a good thing. Relief made me dizzy. "We should get something to cheer her up. You know she won't mind that you told me. And besides, she loves presents."

"I don't have much money," Tasha warned. "I'm pretty broke after the ski trip, and besides, we just gave each other Christmas presents."

"Okay, but we could get her a card now." I took a long sip from my iced coffee. The caffeine shot through my veins. I was feeling more like myself. Now if I could just steer Tasha away from the subject of CJ and Nick, I could really relax.

"I love e-cards," Tasha said. "Let's send her one of those. We can show our support, right? We are the Terribles, after all. Nothing keeps us down." Tasha was staring at her rings.

"Sure, I know what you mean," I said. I cleared my throat. "Hey, guess what, I've got news too."

"Really? Cool, what is it?" She held out her hand. "Do you think this opal is too blah? I might change it for my antique amethyst."

The opal looked gorgeous to me, but I'm not a jewelry expert like Tasha. I shrugged. "I don't know.

But listen, I'm producing a documentary about Fiesta Beach."

Tasha's eyes widened. "Really? Omigod, am I going to be in it? Is it going to be on TV? Maybe Fox or the WB will want it. I can't wait to tell CJ!"

"I don't know about Fox or—"

"Oh, I almost forgot," Tasha interrupted. "Guess who *else* I talked to last night." She looked at me from under her lashes.

Tasha really had the attention span of a gnat—a gnat with ADDH. I jumped easily back into my normal role. "Oh, gee, that's a tough one. Who could it be? Someone who worships you. Someone who is totally obsessed with you—"

Tasha snickered. "It was so awesome to see Chi. Very romantic."

"Don't tell me you guys made out with your parents at home?" I already knew the answer.

"Just a little." Tasha pouted. "Then my mom started in on how it was late. You know how she gets."

"I don't suppose you told Chi about the guys you hooked up with at the lodge."

"Don't ask, don't tell." She laughed and stood up. "Chi knows I don't like to be tied down, and he handles it. Someday, Gen, if you're with a guy, you'll realize that they hate chicks who are clingy and boring. It's better to keep them on their toes."

She squeezed my arm. "That is awesome about your show, Gen. I'm definitely getting a new bikini for Fiesta Beach. And I'll get a pedicure for sure." She paused for breath. "But first, I want to show you these really hot boots. They may be too pink. I can't be sure, so I need your opinion."

Oh well. Maybe we'd talk more about my show when she was less wired and I was feeling more normal. I trotted obediently beside Tasha, who was charging relentlessly toward Nordstrom. She had that faraway look in her eyes that she usually only gets when she talks about skiing or when she's shopping. There's not much else that captures Tash's attention for more than a few seconds.

I was relieved but a little antsy, though I don't know why. I'd gotten away with it. Nick would never breathe a word, so CJ would never know. Good old Gen, that's who I was, dispenser of advice and comfort and advisor to the stars on love and clothes. I was safe. But somehow I didn't feel as great as I thought I would.

Tasha suddenly stopped in her tracks, causing me to crash into a display of purses.

"I forgot to tell you something else."

I picked up a Kate Spade from the floor. "Yeah?" I was only half listening.

"CJ is totally flipping out, because she thinks Nick cheated on her while she was in Cancún."

Of course, Nick and CJ were supposed to be in an open relationship, but to CJ that meant she could hook up with anyone she wanted while Nick was supposed to live like a monk.

I slowly straightened up. "What? How would she know that? I thought she hasn't talked to anyone but you."

"Hello, she can still read e-mails. What else does she have to do?"

I couldn't speak for a second; everything was spinning around me.

"CJ doesn't know who this other girl is, but Kyle Anslow e-mailed that he saw Nick with someone last night," Tasha went on.

"Kyle was probably stoned. CJ shouldn't listen to him," I croaked.

"Well, she is listening to him, and she is pissed," Tasha said. "She's ready to kill the ho if she ever finds out who she is."

I tried to mumble something but my mouth was too dry. I tried to step forward but my foot caught on the carpet. I was lurching around like an extra from *Night of the Living Dead*.

Tasha didn't notice and grabbed my arm with all five dagger-long fake nails. "There they are!" she shrieked, piercing my eardrum.

"*What?*" For a nauseating moment, I thought she was talking about Nick and CJ.

"The boots! Aren't they incredible?" Tasha had pounced on a pair of pink boots and triumphantly waved them under my nose. "Hello, Gen, are you there? What do you think of them?"

"Nice, really nice," I whispered.

"Aren't you blown away? Admit it. You're blown away." She hugged the boots and grinned. I coughed.

"Yeah, that's what I am. Blown away."

Message Board

✉ THIS IS WHY I HATE CERTAIN GIRLS—
007ugo—at 6:23 a.m.

Tasha is like the most spoiled girl on the planet. I know she acts like she is the hottest girl on the planet. So does CJ. They treat men like dirt. You don't think so, queenSheba, but you don't know about them like us older girls do. I think Gen was amazing to be their friend. She must have seen good in them somehow. the rest of us always thought they were the worst skanks (and still think it). CJ didn't mind when she cheated on Nick, but then she got mad when he did the same thing. Totally unfair.

✉ Re: THIS IS WHY I HATE CERTAIN GIRLS—
JUICYFRUIT45—at 11:57 p.m.

You're right, 007ugo, Tasha and CJ don't sound nice at all. They sound like girls I'd be enemies with too. I've tried not to judge, but they sound really mean and conceited to me.

✉ Re: THIS IS WHY I HATE CERTAIN GIRLS—
queenSheba—at 12:15 a.m.

you're forgetting that genesis was supposed to be best

friends with cj and tasha. you can hate them all you want, but she let them down. she kissed nick two times. she didn't have cj's back. it makes me wonder how much she REALLY cared about them. i think girls should be righteous when it comes to their friends. it doesn't matter that cj and tasha make people mad.

CONFESSIONS OF A BOYFRIEND STEALER—
BLOG BY GENESIS BELL

[7TH ENTRY]

You gotta understand that I'd never messed up with CJ and Tasha before. I'd always been "righteous" with them. Yeah, they had their flaws, but we were always tight, no matter what. I accepted them, and more important, I always thought they accepted me. This was the first time I'd made such a huge mistake with the Terribles.

You'd think I would be a basket case after Tasha dropped her little bombshell, but I was numb. I went through the motions of saying goodbye as she dropped me off, promising to call CJ to find out more dirt on this alleged "other woman," promising to try to rush over to see CJ before her rash was cured, and last but not least, promising to send the get-well e-card.

Oh yeah. I definitely should have been a basket case, but I was too stunned. Numbskull that I was, I never dreamed that anyone would spot Nick and me together. I guess I thought we were invisible, just like the kid who closes his eyes during hide-and-seek and really thinks no one sees him. Idiot, I thought foggily as I flung open the front door.

Luckily it was just Anslow, the local zomboid, who'd seen us, or I'd be in serious trouble.

I walked into my house and right into a battle. Voices were raised to harpy level. It was Shay versus Angela, facing each other like gunslingers, hands on hips, carefully blow-dried hair bouncing around their carefully made-up faces. They were circling a very odd-looking plastic statue. I think it was supposed to be the three wise men and some lambs, but I couldn't be sure.

The whole thing was freaky. I was quickly coming out of my Nick-and-CJ-induced daze. My family can be better than electroshock therapy.

I stared at Angela. She looked different but I didn't have time to figure out why.

"Mother, you can't do this. I'm warning you, I'll call Dr. Vadd," Shay thundered.

This was serious. Dr. Vadd was a holistic therapist who believed in past-life regressions. If you annoyed or offended him, you'd find out that in a past life you were the humpbacked village idiot who lived in the tower eating nothing but mice and mildew. For a New Age guy, he could be mean.

I tried to slink by to my bedroom, hoping they wouldn't see me, but no such luck.

"Genesis agrees with me." Shay glared, daring me to argue. "You've gone way over the edge. You need help, Mother."

"You don't know what you're talking about, Shay. Obviously your heart isn't open to the Lord. If you'd try to invite Him in, you'd feel different." My mother was trying to sound sweet and gentle, but she was gritting her teeth. The effect was not exactly saintly.

"This is so stupid. I can't believe you're going to let them dunk you in dirty old water and ruin your hair and makeup," Shay said, trying to sound reasonable.

I stared at my mother, this time taking in her appearance. She was wearing a long white robe and sandals. In contrast, she was fully made up and her hair was carefully done. The effect was disorienting, sort of Video Vixen meets Prophet in the Desert.

"What's going on?" Like I wanted to know, like I had a choice.

"She's flipped," Shay burst out. "She's so desperate to hook up with Creepy Kenny that she's decided to be baptized. He wants her soul to be purified before he can consider getting *intimate* with her." She made a gagging noise.

My mother narrowed her eyes and jutted her jaw. She was flexing her hands and shifting from foot to foot. I could easily see her in the ring at WrestleMania.

"That's just jealousy, pure and simple. You're pea green with it, Shay, because I've found true, deep,

Christian love. If you met a man like Kenny, you wouldn't be talking like that." Her fake Southern accent was getting stronger.

"If I met a man like Kenny—" Shay pounded on her forehead and let out a shriek of rage and frustration. Then she squared her shoulders and spun on her heel like a soldier. "I'm calling Dr. Vadd tomorrow. I've had it." Dramatically, she pointed to the plastic statue at her feet. "If you don't move this nasty thing, I swear I'll burn it in the fireplace."

She raced off to her bedroom, slamming the door behind her. Hard to believe she's twenty-two. She should be over the tantrum stage by now. My mother swooped down and embraced the statue.

"Don't you worry, sweeties," she crooned to it. "I won't let her hurt my shepherds and lambie-kins." With that, she picked up the statue and stormed to her room. She too slammed the door behind her.

My stomach twisted a little. Crap. If this went on much longer, Genesis, the Bell family bouncer, would have to step in. Couldn't stupid Shay see that she should be patient with Angela? Making fun of the fact that Angela thought she was in love would just make her more stubborn. Shay should at least *pretend* to respect Angela's feelings.

The important thing was that the drama and weirdness be kept down to a manageable level. Damn, it was hard being the bouncer sometimes.

Maybe Kenny would go back to his wife.

With everyone gone, I suddenly noticed the clean

living room. Even the furniture was dusted, and I saw vacuum tracks on the carpet. Had to be Kenny's influence on my mother. I guess cleanliness really is next to godliness—but whatever.

I slammed my own bedroom door, because I, after all, had something real to stress over. I sank onto the bed and picked at my chipped nail polish. CJ was going to be on the warpath. That was a given. That girl is a pit bull. She really is a terrible Terrible. Once in junior high she discovered that someone had written *CJ is a big slut* on the girls' bathroom wall (CJ doesn't freak over verbal rumors but goes ballistic over anything in writing). Well, she couldn't rest until she hunted down the culprit (she interrogated a bunch of girls until someone finally snapped). She very quickly had the girl who did it blubbering and scrubbing the wall.

For a size two, CJ can be really intimidating. She's a lot more intense than fluffy Tasha. So should I worry about CJ and me going at each other, *SmackDown!* style, or should I worry about CJ crying and going Ricki Lake on me about betrayals and backstabbers? Crap, it wasn't fair. The one time I do something the slightest bit exciting, I get into trouble. I know, I know, it was my own fault, and I didn't want to hurt my friend, but somehow I still felt like a victim.

Yeah, women like CJ, Shay, and my mother get away with murder on a regular basis. I remember when my sister had four guys give her engagement rings within two weeks. None of the guys found out about each other. Not only didn't she marry any of them, but she also got to keep all the rings. Three were real diamonds, and the cubic zirconia wasn't cheap.

My mother was once responsible for making some totally gay guy fall madly in love with her. He ended up in therapy (for years), while my mom wrote it off as a "special experience."

All I did was exchange a few innocent kisses with a friend. It's not like we had sex or anything. Not even close. Damn.

For a luxurious second, I let myself fantasize about Nick and how great it was kissing him. There's something about a round bed that inspires hot fantasies.

I reached down to the floor for a bottle of silver nail polish I'd snagged from my sister's room. Nothing looks worse than peeling, chipped red polish. I was too lazy to remove the old stuff and decided to layer the silver over it.

My mother knocked on my door and marched in without waiting for my invite. I almost poured the polish onto the bed. She was still in her Ten Commandments robe and sandals.

"I just wanted y'all to know that I'm leaving now. Don't wait up for me either." She was flipping her hair like a crazed person, and her cheeks were red. Obviously, she was still pissed at my sister.

For a second, I actually thought of telling her about me, Nick, and CJ. Then sanity kicked in. She simply wouldn't see the big deal, or she might take me window-shopping at Gucci (that's her cure-all for everything).

Okay, I gotta be fair. Angela once did help me through a crisis. When I was eight, Cathy Lee Parsons had a big sleepover party and invited everyone but me. I was crushed, and Angela ended up taking me to Disney for a whole day. Sure, one of her boyfriends went with us and treated us, but it did take my mind off the sleepover.

That was nice, but it was eight years ago. I didn't think Goofy and Mickey would help right now.

Angela stared at me, a shocked expression spreading across her face. Omigod, she somehow knew about Nick and *was* horrified. Kenny's morality had rubbed off on her. I doubt she'd be offering Disney today. My pulse went crazy.

"Genesis Bell, I can't believe my eyes. You're applying new polish over old polish. How many times do I have to tell you that a good manicure is the best tool for success in life? Think of it as one of the Five Commandments." She began ticking them off on her fingers. "Thou shalt remove the old polish, thou shalt condition, thou shalt do the cuticles, thou shalt apply a primer coat, and thou shalt apply new polish." She giggled. "See what my newfound religion is doing for me?"

I nodded obediently. I was almost hysterical with relief. "You're right. I have sinned. I'll never do it again." I kissed the nail polish bottle for dramatic effect.

"Are you making fun of me and Kenny?" she demanded.

I shook my head and put the bottle on the floor. "I was kidding. I was just going to wish you a happy baptism."

She was mollified. "Well, thanks, sweetie. I really appreciate your support. At least I can count on you. Your sister is simply impossible. Neither of you have even met Kenny yet."

My mom looked genuinely wounded. I was floored. I'd never seen her like this before.

"So you really dig him, huh? Is it serious?"

She grew misty-eyed. "Yes, we are two halves of the same soul, Genesis. We just have some problems to sort out."

I tried to appear wise and knowing. "Divine stuff, huh?"

"No, his ex-wife. Well, she'll be his ex, once she accepts the Lord's word."

This mystified me, since I couldn't picture Jesus getting in the middle of Kenny's marital dispute. Luckily, I was too smart to say so out loud.

MESSAGE BOARD

✉ GENESIS AND HER FAMILY—JUICYFRUIT45—AT 9:21 A.M.

Her mom and sister are so amazing in a weird, funny way. I think they'd be a blast to be around. Being a born-again is pretty serious. I know 'cause my aunt got into it for a while. Somehow it's hard to picture Gen's mom as the born-again type. ;-)

✉ Re: genesis and her family—queen-Sheba—at 11:03 a.m.

gen's family is such a bad influence. i can't imagine growing up in that kind of household. no wonder she said her friends mattered so much. but that makes you ask why she screwed them over. i'd have cried myself to sleep over betraying my best friend! juicyfruit45 and 007ugo, you guys amaze me because you blow off what happened with gen and nick!

✉ Re: genesis and her family—007ugo—at 12:01 p.m.

Give me a break! Gen shouldn't have shed one tear over this situation. All she did was KISS a guy. CJ and Tasha have done much worse. Believe me, queen-Sheba, you just don't know. I heard that Tasha once made out with some girl's boyfriend RIGHT in front of the girl and everyone else at some party . . . then she broke up with the guy a week later! Tasha KNEW this girl was totally in love and didn't care. CJ and Tasha are EVIL. But enough about them for now. I admit that Gen's family is pretty crazy.

MOST RECENT ENTRIES CALENDAR

VIEW FRIENDS LINKS PHOTOS

05/04 10:02:01

CONFESSIONS OF A BOYFRIEND STEALER—
BLOG BY GENESIS BELL

[8TH ENTRY]

Listen, I know my family isn't exactly the Brady Bunch; heck, I doubt they'd even be allowed in the Brady neighborhood. I know CJ and Tasha aren't angels either. I was the one to blame, and I know it. But I just wanted to erase the whole Nick episode.

← →

It was peaceful once my mother left. My sister was sulking in her room with Enya turned up. But Enya, even loud, is soothing.

For some reason, I was starting to feel better about the Nick, CJ, and Genesis triangle. It would blow over. School would start soon, and CJ would get so caught up in all the new gossip and drama that she'd forget the other woman rumor. I felt good enough to send CJ a get-well e-card. It was *Hello Kitty* and too sweet for words. I typed FEEL BETTER! WE MISS YOU! THE

TERRIBLES. Short, I know, but writing much more would ruin my mood.

A peaceful feeling was spreading inside me as I returned to piling silver polish on top of my chipped red. Maybe I'd order in a pizza and write out some notes on my documentary. Maybe I'd find some (unattached) guy to go to Fiesta Beach with me. Or maybe I'd actually hook up at the party. Maybe lots of guys would chase me, just like my heroine in *Alien Love*. Maybe I'd become one of those Fiesta Beach legends.

I know. Delusional. It was just cool to think about it. My nails were dry, so I stretched out on the bed.

I must have fallen asleep for at least an hour. I was dreaming about being in a hot tub with a gorgeous guy who looked like Nick (but it wasn't him, I swear). It was dark when I awoke to Shay yelling my name. She stuck her head in my room and hit the lights.

She almost blinded me. I wanted to kill her.

"Tasha's on the phone," she announced. God, her voice was loud. "It's almost five-thirty. Are you going to order us something to eat?" My sister is so used to people waiting on her that she never dreams of picking up the phone herself. Of course, actually preparing a meal with her own little hands is completely out of the question.

My mouth felt dry and icky, and my eyes would barely open. My sister was jamming the cell phone against my ear and tapping her foot impatiently.

"Hurry up. I'm starving. I want vegetable and double mushroom from Pizza Hut."

She knows I hate mushrooms, but she always insists that I just pick them off. She refuses to listen to me when I tell her the pizza still has a mushroomy taste and smell.

I squinted at her. "Sheesh, could you give me a second? I just want a quick word with Tash."

She snorted and left.

Tasha's voice blasted into my ear. She was almost louder than Shay. "Guess what! We're meeting at the Happy Buddha tomorrow at five. CJ's rash is clearing up fast with this new medicine, and she can't wait to tell us all about Nick and his ho."

I stuttered something moronic, then mutely listened to Tasha babble for the next few seconds before finally hanging up.

If only I could have thought of a decent excuse. If only Tasha had given me more warning. If only I could have managed to postpone the stupid dinner.

If only . . .

← →

I usually love the Happy Buddha. It's one of the best things about this town. They serve the greatest vegetable spring rolls and fried wontons in the world, and they play alternative music by new regional talent. The décor is hip and artsy, but best of all, the waiters are always nice to teens, unlike at most restaurants.

That night, I trudged in looking like the Happy Buddha's unhappiest customer. It was windy and chilly outside, a big contrast to the warm restaurant. I rubbed my cold hands together. I so didn't want to face CJ. I so didn't want to hear all about the nasty ho who tried to steal CJ's man. The hostess, this gorgeous girl all in black with like a twenty-inch waist and hair to her butt, smiled at me.

"Your party's waiting for you," she said.

Nowhere to run. Nowhere to hide. I followed her through packed tables with Iron Lucinda wafting in through the speakers. Usually when I hear Iron Lucinda, an awesome local emo band, I feel very spiritual, but not tonight.

The hostess led me to the back, and sure enough, Tasha and CJ were already seated.

They had their heads together, and I could see their lips moving at high speed. CJ looked normal to me, except maybe she was wearing a little more makeup than usual. For a fleeting second, I thought of running for the door, but they both looked up. Trapped.

Tasha waved like a demented person.

"Hurry up, Gen. You're moving like a senior citizen. Get over here." Tasha was practically bouncing in her seat.

CJ was glaring menacingly into her iced tea. "We've got to talk, Genesis. This is serious." She looked up at me, her eyes glittering. "We need you. Three heads are better than two."

I plunked down into the empty chair. A pupu platter was on the table. Tasha had filled her plate, while CJ was dissecting a tiny, lone spare rib. They weren't touching these fried crab things, and I didn't blame them. They're barf.

"Did Tasha tell you about my documentary?" I asked, hoping to stall the dreaded conversation. "It's going to be hot. I thought you guys would want to help me think of—"

CJ fluttered her fingers at me. "Yeah, yeah, I heard. It sounds great, but we have more important things to discuss now. We were just figuring out how we're going to kill that ho Sherryn Feldman. If you have any ideas, feel free." Her rash was totally gone, and she looked flawlessly beautiful, as usual.

Damn. I grabbed a couple of fried wontons and plopped them on my plate. "Sherryn?" I almost choked on my wonton. "I don't get it."

CJ narrowed her eyes at some faraway object. "I didn't either, Gen. That's the problem. I caught Sherryn practically feeling Nick up in the hallway right before break. She claimed she was trying to sell raffle tickets for theater, but I know better."

CJ has this delicate little china-doll face, which is totally misleading. Her eyes were pure ice, and she looked more than a little homicidal.

"You know Nick, he likes to kid around. He was pretending to steal her stupid raffle tickets. She was tickling him to get the tickets back, but it was obviously part of her master plan."

I swallowed hard and tried to keep my face calm. Had I chewed first?

Tasha shook her head and dipped a spare rib in plum sauce. "You should have like kicked her butt then, CJ."

"I know, I know. I totally regret it, but I didn't think Sherryn would really have the nerve to go after Nick." She tossed her head imperiously. She was, after all, CJ Thompson, resident goddess of Jamaica Plains High. She also was not the type to see the irony in the situation: her getting all pissy because a girl dared try to snag her boyfriend. Some people (though not Tash or me) would say CJ was getting a taste of her own medicine.

"I say we put Nair in her shampoo, or maybe spray-paint the words *tramp* and *bitch* all over her locker," Tasha said. She made stabbing motions with her chewed-on spare rib.

"She loves that stupid little car she drives. Maybe her tires will accidentally get slashed." CJ cackled.

The hair on my neck stood up. This was turning too Jerry Springer.

"You don't know for sure it's Sherryn. You don't even know for sure Nick was cheating," I pointed out. Man, did I sound rational, but my heart was thudding really fast. Speaking was getting harder and harder, since my tongue seemed to be swelling in my mouth.

My stomach started to feel a little sour too. It was like my worst fears were turning into reality. CJ was after blood. Okay, not my blood, but it was still scary.

"It's true," CJ assured me. "Everyone knows Nick was with some girl. Someone said it was Sherryn. They were totally sure of it too."

Everyone? How could that be possible? I thought only one lone idiot, Kyle Anslow, had spotted Nick and me at the Blue Circle. And how did poor Sherryn Feldman get the blame? She and I looked nothing alike. She's tall with long, wild black hair and is as exotic as they come. I'm Jan Brady, remember? Sherryn's total opposite. The gossip machine was out of control and creating its own version of reality. Believe me, this was standard Jamaica Plains High crap.

"We've got to get her. Girls like her are dangerous once they have power." Tasha sounded really serious.

"You're right," CJ said. "Sherryn is way out of line."

"What do you mean 'girls like her'?" The conversation was moving so fast that I was having a hard time keeping up. My voice sounded squeaky.

Our waitress materialized at that point to refill our drinks. We clammed up. She didn't ask for our orders and left quickly.

CJ's eyes bored into mine. "I admit Sherryn is beautiful in her own way, but she's not one of us. She should stick to other theater geeks."

Tasha nudged me. "Gen, c'mon. Sherryn and her crew are always acting like they're so much better than us. She's got a nerve going after one of our guys."

"She's a major slut, and she's going to really, really regret messing with my man." CJ glanced first at Tasha and then at me. "We'll do her car first and then her locker. Agreed?"

Tasha nodded eagerly. She was on the edge of her seat as if ready to rush right out with a sharp knife and a paintbrush.

Stop them! I told myself. Don't let poor Sherryn take the fall. You're a Terrible, Genesis Bell. CJ will kill you, but you'll get over it.

CJ once stole Tasha's boyfriend and vice versa. True, they nearly ripped each other to shreds (I shuddered), but they finally made up. In the end, the Terribles always rule.

My stomach was clenching and twisting, and I was actually feeling nauseated. I was the bad guy. It was written all over my face, I'm sure. They just couldn't see it.

I was the one who'd locked lips with hot, hot Nick Pilates.

"Gen, you're not saying anything. How come?" CJ said, offering me the perfect chance to be honest.

I couldn't say it, not even to save Sherryn. A coward, that's what I am. I prayed that a tornado would swoop up the Happy Buddha. Only a natural disaster would stop CJ when she was like this.

I had to try to divert her, though, at least in a subtle way.

"I just don't get why you're not mad at Nick. That's all." I cleared my throat. Okay, I was serving Nick up on a platter, but he could defend himself better than Sherryn.

"Oh, I'm pissed at him," CJ said. "But, you know." She shrugged. She and Tasha exchanged looks.

I didn't get it, of course.

"Guys are weak," Tasha supplied. "They can't help being dogs. Girls are supposed to know better." She waved her hands around. God, she had a lot of rings.

I was about to point out how unfair that was when CJ said in her supersweet tone, "Maybe you'll understand someday, Gen."

And then Tasha patted my hand. "You're bound to get a boyfriend in the next couple of years."

Up until then, I was feeling so guilty and so anxious that I thought I was going to heave my wontons. But now a new emotion was ripping through to the surface. I was getting pissed, which had a calming effect on my stomach.

Tash and CJ were talking to me like I was a lame-o, like I was wearing earflaps and flood pants. Like I had to ride a special bus.

"I can see why Nick was tempted," CJ said. "In a low-class way, Sherryn is sexy."

Tasha nodded. "Girls like Sherryn can steal any guy away. Temporarily." She smirked. "Except for Chi. He's totally mine."

"You are so lucky, Tash. You've got such a slave boy." CJ took a teensy bite of the same spare rib that had been on her plate when I arrived. "As for Sherryn, that bitch is toast."

CJ suddenly pulled her PDA from her pocket. She looked at it and quickly IM'd something back. "Nick," she said with a smug smile. "I let him know I was home this morning. Of course, I haven't told him I know all about him and the Slut." She put her PDA away. "He'll figure it out after we nail Sherryn."

"Smart," Tasha said. "Make him sweat. When he sees what you do to Sherryn, I bet you he never cheats again." She giggled. "He might think you'd trash his 'vette."

"One night alone with me, and he'll soon forget about the Slut," CJ said confidently.

"He was probably drunk, or he'd have never hooked up with her," Tasha added.

"I know. Him and his gross homemade vodka. No wonder the Slut got her hooks into him." CJ rolled her eyes.

"She's pathetic," Tasha said. "Girls like that are like desperate. They'll do anything—"

"Will you guys shut up! *I'm* the Slut!" I didn't mean to shout, but the words just seemed to explode from my lips.

I didn't know I was about to confess everything. It just sort of happened. I went off like a can of Coke does when you shake it up too much. Everything was gushing out of me.

CJ and Tasha sat there staring. I was afraid to look around the restaurant. I'm sure the whole room was watching us now. Out of the corner of my eye, I caught this old couple in matching sweats at a nearby table gawking at me. I felt like a total dweeb. But I was really mad, since all of that trash the Terribles were talking about Sherryn was really about me.

It was *go* time. I had to tell the truth. Half of me was ready to pass out; the other half was almost happy. It was time to puncture their little balloons.

"I was with Nick," I blurted. "Not *with*-with him, but we went out, and—"

There was a moment of utter silence. I was sweating big time. I could feel my armpits turning gross. Was CJ going for her knife? Should I make a run for it?

Tasha and CJ looked at each other and burst out laughing. They weren't just giggling. Oh no. They were snorting and slapping their knees and rocking in their chairs. The full monty.

Of all the reactions I imagined I might get, that wasn't one of them.

"Listen, guys, I'm not kidding—"

They were still laughing like stupid hyenas. I wanted to kill them. I grabbed CJ's arm hard and said, "I mean it. I was with Nick. I really was. We went to the Blue—"

Tasha interrupted me. "Stop, we know what you're doing." She again exploded into snorts of laughter. "You're afraid we'll get into trouble if we go after Sherryn, so you're making up these wild-ass lies. It's cute, trying to protect us."

CJ pulled her arm from my grasp. "We're not going to hurt Sherryn, just teach her a lesson." She rolled her eyes. "Chill, will you?"

"I'm serious." I wasn't sure if I wanted to scream or cry. This situation truly sucked. I was a Terrible. I could be dangerous too. Didn't they get that?

"Right," CJ said. "You and Nick."

"But it's the truth!" I wanted to stamp my foot. "I'm the one he went out with. I'm the one he kissed! Not Sherryn!"

"Stop screaming, Gen. We know what you're up to." CJ paused. "So give it a rest."

"You are so crazy," Tasha said, wiping her eyes.

"Listen," CJ said soothingly, as if to a lunatic, "what if we promise not to slash her tires, huh? We'll just spray-paint her locker. That's not a big deal, right? It will just get the message across."

She nudged Tasha, who nodded eagerly and said, "Sure, just calm down. You're turning bright red."

"You guys—" I started, then stopped. Nothing. I wasn't getting through. It was hopeless. I was shaking, and everything was spinning. Now I was hyperventilating. I wasn't sure I'd make it out of the restaurant without collapsing.

But I got up, trying to look dignified. It wasn't easy, considering my audience was practically rolling in the aisles.

"I have to go home. My mother and Shay are having a crisis," I said, which was the truth, after all.

I could not wait to get out of there. Despite my shaky legs, I rushed out of the restaurant, not bothering to look back at Tasha and CJ. The cold wind outside was a rough slap in the face, but I didn't care.

I was relieved that I'd parked Shay's white Jeep close to the restaurant, so I could peel out as fast as possible. At first I was too upset to do more than drive. My face felt scorching, and my hands were trembling.

My best friends had laughed in my face. I switched the radio on, then off. I had to concentrate. I may be pond scum because I went out with my best friend's man, but they're morons. Jerks. Real friends would have wanted to kick my ass.

I was a Terrible, right? Or was I? CJ and Tash were acting like I was something else, like maybe I was just the hired help and a Terrible wannabe.

I hit the gas and passed a line of slow cars to my right. I zipped in front of a slowpoke SUV, whose driver honked and flipped me off. It felt good to flip him back. It felt good to get ahead of the crowd. At least they had to pay attention to me.

In all the movies I've seen and all the books I've read, the femme fatale always leaves women crying and men wanting more. I've never heard about her victims laughing their asses off.

By the time I pulled up to my house, I realized I was pissed off *and* starving. I hadn't gotten the chance to really eat at the Happy Buddha, and despite my psychologically scarring trauma, I needed food. I've never been one of those girls who can live on Chiclets, lettuce leaves, and fruit-flavored bottled water.

I was fantasizing about microwaving some mac and cheese and maybe adding some jalapeños and olives to the mix when I noticed a strange car parked in front of our house. It was an old sedan. I parked Shay's Jeep behind it and tried to figure out who was here. None of Shay's guys would be caught dead driving something so senior citizen. Angela's friends drive either pickups or muscle cars.

My stomach growled, and I suddenly remembered we had a stash of leftover Christmas cookies and fudge. Hey, I was super emotionally drained. I needed extra sustenance. I opened the door cautiously. If my mom was talking to some salesman about our financial planning or our insurance needs, I didn't want to be around. I just hoped whoever it was would leave soon. I was in a *Blair Witch* mood (which I'm sure you'd agree was perfectly understandable). I just wanted to curl up with my mac and cheese and watch my favorite bad-ass movie.

I walked into the living room and about keeled over. Angela was sitting on the couch holding hands with a man wearing a *plaid* shirt. If you knew Angela as I do and were familiar with her incredibly picky taste in what she calls style, you'd have been blown away too. My mother's men usually wore Armani or at least genuine leather Harley jackets. I always thought she was allergic to plaid shirts, which in her mind were the equivalent of the dreaded denim overalls.

The man and my mother were watching TV, and I swear it was some PAX thing or 700 Club or whatever. This was too, too creepy. And the living room was neat and clean—again. Was this getting to be a trend?

My mother beamed at me, bleached white teeth shining. She sprang to her feet.

"Gen, you're home. This is just perfect. You can meet Kenny."

The man in plaid stood up and walked over to shake my hand. "You can call me Ken if you want," he said. He grinned at me. "Only your mother calls me Kenny."

"It's a sign of affection," my mother said, batting her eyes. "I only use nicknames for my favorite people, don't I, Genesis?"

I shook his hand, not bothering to answer her.

"I hope you don't mind that I stopped by," Kenny said. "I brought over some fried chicken. There's a lot left over in the kitchen. Help yourself."

My stomach grumbled. "Okay, sure. Thanks."

"Kenny brought KFC instead of one of those cheaper types," my mother sang. "Isn't that sweet?"

KFC? I guessed old Kenny did like the simple life. Angela usually only accepted gourmet carry-out. Of course, I love the Colonel (www.kfc.com), so Kenny scored big points in my book.

"Well, uh, I'm pretty hungry, so I'll go get myself some chicken."

"Just make sure you pull off the fried skin, Genesis. It's full of fat. And no gravy," my mother lectured.

"Leave her alone, honey." Kenny sat on the couch

and pulled my mother down beside him. "It was nice to meet you, Genesis. By the way, I like your name, but that's probably no surprise." He winked at me.

I smiled a little despite myself. "Well, uh, thanks for the food."

Maybe Kenny wasn't so bad. Except for the plaid and the religious stuff, he seemed like a pretty normal guy. I was surprised.

I walked into the kitchen and saw that Kenny had brought a big spread. A huge bucket of chicken was on the counter with a ton of side dishes: mashed potatoes, baked beans, macaroni and cheese, biscuits, and even apple pie.

I loaded up my plate, and no, I did not take my mother's advice about the chicken. How gross would that be to rip greasy skin off cooked flesh? Not to mention that naked meat would taste like barf. And of course, I poured on the gravy.

I tried to block out the sounds of my mother and Kenny and God TV. I grabbed a bottle of Coke and sat down to stuff myself.

". . . lucky to have such a sweet daughter. Nothing matters more than our loved ones. . . . Family and friends are such blessings . . . ," I heard Kenny say before the TV drowned him out.

I winced and took a slug of Coke. Food was clearing my head. I started feeling a little silly, like I'd overreacted in the restaurant. I also started feeling more than a little guilty (maybe it was Kenny's influence), because CJ and Tasha were my best friends. Of course they didn't believe me, because I hadn't told them the entire story. Of course they didn't believe me, because we were so close, the Terribles forever. They wouldn't have expected me to betray CJ. *I* wouldn't have expected me to betray CJ, let alone to confess to it. The Terribles had been a major part of my life and I couldn't just erase that. Just thinking of how crappy junior high would have been without them made me shudder.

I actually met Tasha first. I'd been at Jamaica Plains High for about three weeks when I walked into the girls' bathroom and found her crying because her genuine opal pierced earring had fallen off and rolled down into the bathroom vent. She was kneeling and trying to poke a pen at it through the slats. It was pretty hopeless, and I felt bad for her. Plus, the girls watching from the sinks were actually smirking over Tasha's dilemma. Later on, I'd find out why.

So I knelt down next to her and removed the vent cover, using a big paper clip to unscrew the nails (I learned resourcefulness from growing up in the Bell household). I got her earring out, and she was so happy that she immediately invited me to have lunch with her, even though we'd never even been introduced and I was a new kid who didn't fit in anywhere. I was just amazed that this gorgeous girl wearing designer clothes was so nice.

Tasha introduced me to CJ at lunch, and the three of us became almost instant friends. I couldn't believe they wanted to hang out with me. Of course, I very quickly learned that they had no other friends because they both had a tendency to steal other girls' guys or crushes. They were pretty merciless and didn't seem to notice how many people they left crying in their wake. The girls in our class totally hated them; the guys totally wanted them.

I always figured CJ and Tasha couldn't help themselves. It wasn't their fault they were so beautiful. I blamed the guys. They could have showed some self-control, right? Someone had to give CJ and Tasha a break, and that someone was me. I was their friend. I was one of them. I was a Terrible.

I shouldn't have run out of the restaurant without giving them a blow-by-blow about Nick and me. I should have told them about watching *Scary Movie 2* and going to see Leaden and even about us meeting the sleazy girl with the roots. No one could make up that many juicy, weird details. They would have known I wasn't lying.

I know at first I was hoping to hide the Nick hookup, but that was a huge mistake. If the Terribles had one redeeming quality, it was that at least we were honest with each other. I could always count on CJ and Tasha to tell me when I had something in my teeth or needed a haircut. We had to keep it real, or our friendship would have had no point whatsoever.

My little display at the Happy Buddha had been

lame at best. I would have laughed at me too. Could I really blame CJ and Tasha?

I took a long drink of Coke. Then I ate some chicken and some potatoes. Food always raises my spirits.

This could be fixed. All I had to do was sit the Terribles down and very seriously, very forcefully explain the truth to them: that I, Genesis Bell, a Terrible, had swapped spit with Nick Pilates and had enjoyed it.

Maybe I would leave that last part out.

Anyway, CJ and Tasha would finally believe me, and we'd all get over it. They'd apologize (for laughing at me) and I'd apologize (for hooking up with Nick). We'd be the Terrible Three again. This was just an ugly misunderstanding. Nick simply happened to be caught in the middle of it.

Nick. Damn. He was going to be so busted. I had to at least warn him. That was the fair and decent thing to do.

At least I wasn't Sherryn, though. CJ absolutely hated her. I was feeling a lot better. Everything would be okay.

I mixed a little apple pie into some mashed potatoes, which is really awesome, despite how it sounds, and then I heard a familiar voice. I put down my fork.

A shudder went down my spine. I swallowed hard. My Zen mood dissolved—it was so unfair. Damn. Shay was home.

Kenny was here.

Crap. All hell was about to break loose.

Message Board

✉ Totally Bad—queenSheba—at 10:32 p.m.

that was a really horrible scene at the Happy Buddha. if i were gen, i'd have been soooo embarrassed that i'd have hidden in my room forever. first she was trying to admit something horrible. then they just made fun of her!

✉ Re: Totally Bad—juicyfruit45—at 10:36 p.m.

Poor Gen. I know she wanted to forgive her friends and make things good between them, but I seriously think I'd have been crushed by what happened at the Happy budda. you are so right, queensheba.

✉ Re: Totally Bad—007ugo—at 10:39 p.m.

Cj and Tasha are so nasty. They can't picture any other girl attracting a guy, especially if he belongs to one of them. They think gen and the rest of us are just losers or something. gen was a really good friend for wanting to make up with cj and tasha after the way they acted. You see that, right, queenSheba?

yeah, but gen started the whole problem when she messed with nick. not to be harsh, but she only had herself to blame. plus, she shouldn't have been worrying about her sister and kenny and everything. her own life was a total disaster! Sometimes, you have to put your family out of your mind!

MOST RECENT ENTRIES   CALENDAR

VIEW FRIENDS   LINKS   PHOTOS

05/04 06:03:13

CONFESSIONS OF A BOYFRIEND STEALER— BLOG BY GENESIS BELL

[9TH ENTRY]

Unfortunately, my family does not come with a mute button. If any of you have figured out how to tune them out when they're at full volume, please tell me. I knew from experience that escape was not an option.

← →

I told myself not to get up and referee. I had enough going on in my own life. I just wanted to eat and zone out.

I resumed carefully mashing my potatoes and apple pie.

I had to think about what was important. I would not be seeing Nick Pilates again—alone. Nick of the sexy lips and hot kisses. Nick, who was now totally off limits. I was okay with that. Really, I swear I was. Sure, my lips tingled at the memories . . . but the main thing was getting us three Terribles back on track—

Voices again. My mother's was a little raised. Was she getting pissed? I heard Kenny's soft rumble, and Shay's petulant, deep-throated whine.

I jabbed the fork faster into the pile on my plate.

A few words filtered through. ". . . need privacy . . . feeling really sick . . ." That was Shay. She was the loudest, naturally.

Then: ". . . sorry . . . should be leaving . . ." Kenny.

Then my mother: ". . . ridiculous . . ."

Raised voices again. Then footsteps.

Don't listen, don't listen, I told myself. I was like the Cowardly Lion in *The Wizard of Oz,* chanting "I do believe in spooks, I do believe in spooks," just because he didn't want to be ripped to pieces like the Scarecrow. I could totally relate to him.

So far, I hadn't heard any actual screams or heavy thuds or gunshots. The footsteps were getting closer. I nearly jumped out of my chair and then looked down at my food, which I'd pretty much pulverized. I dumped it into the sink and turned on the water.

Shay sailed through the kitchen without speaking and slammed her door behind her.

Nice.

I got up to check on Mr. and Ms. Born-Again, just to make sure they weren't missing any body parts or weren't comatose and bleeding on the floor.

My mother was pacing around the living room.

"I'll kill her," she intoned.

Neither she nor Kenny noticed me yet. I started to open my mouth but thought better of it.

Kenny was still seated but was leaning forward as if ready to lasso my mother back to the sofa.

"Angela, we have to be patient. Every trial the Lord puts before us can be overcome with love and understanding. Besides, your Shay was feeling poorly. We shouldn't judge her too harshly." Kenny was sincere, I could tell. He sounded anxious and worried, the poor guy.

My mother put her hands on her hips. "She had the nerve to ask when you were leaving!"

They still hadn't spotted me in the doorway. They were too caught up in the aftermath of Hurricane Shay.

Kenny held out a hand. "Please sit, Angela. Shay is obviously an emotional young woman. She needs our consideration."

"She needs a kick in the butt," my mother said. The fact that she used the word *butt* instead of *ass* shows you how far she'd go to play up to Kenny. "She wasn't raised to act like a heathen."

My mother was getting creepy. The Southern accent was one thing, but using the word *heathen*? What was next for Angela Bell? Tent revivals and speaking in tongues? I shuddered and slinked back to the kitchen.

"She's faking being sick," my mother ranted. "She's just being miserable and jealous."

"Then she must be truly troubled," Kenny countered. "Her sensitive soul must be aching. She *really* needs our understanding." Boy, Shay sure had sucked

Kenny in. I could hear the emotion in his voice. He was seriously upset.

I took that as my cue to split. Talking about Shay's soul was actually making my flesh crawl; plus, she'd flip if she heard Kenny defending her. I had to talk to her. If she would just chill, this entire episode would blow over. Otherwise, everything might get out of hand. And it was my job as bouncer to keep the patrons from tearing up the place.

Despite her claim of being in love, my mother would soon tire of Kenny, and she and Shay could go back to being *bestest friends ever.* Or even better, Hilton sister wannabes.

I didn't knock, knowing Shay would tell me to get lost. I opened her door and discreetly squeezed inside, trying not to make any noise. I didn't want to alert my mom and Kenny to my whereabouts.

Shay was on the floor doing elaborate stomach crunches. Seriously, if you want those washboard abs everyone worships, you have to exercise like ten hours a day.

"What do you want?" Miss Sensitive Soul asked. Her stomach was perfect, I had to give her that. Her personality was another thing.

I sat on her bed uninvited. She had this awesome, very expensive black silk spread on it, which felt really good. I couldn't remember which boyfriend had given it to her. "I think you should cut Mom and Kenny some slack. You're making too big a deal about it."

She crunched some more before speaking. Watching her made my stomach ache.

"You don't understand. Mom is being the biggest phony about this religious stuff, and it makes me sick." She panted a few times and then continued. "Plus the guy is weird."

"But if you keep pushing it, Mom will end up marrying Kenny, just out of spite."

"Mom's let me—*us*—down, Gen," she panted. "She's pretending she's someone else. I don't even know her anymore. She used to be honest in relationships."

She did? Were we talking about Angela Bell, the Queen of the Game? The Mistress of Manipulation? The only new things I saw in her relationship with Kenny were this love stuff and the church angle.

My sister was feeling left out or left behind. Not that she'd admit it in a million years. If I calmed her down, she wouldn't do anything too trailer trash. I hoped. I had enough chaos and crap in my life right now.

"Listen, why don't you just ask if Kenny has a hot, rich, religious friend? Then you and Mom can hang out more, and you'll see for yourself that she's okay."

Shay snorted and made a face.

"Puh-lease! How lame do you think I am? I don't need to be fixed up."

She crunched faster. "Besides, it's Mom who has the problem, not me."

Well, that didn't work. Maybe I could embarrass her into getting a grip.

"It's just that you've got them all worked up, Shay. Kenny's about ready to pray over you. He thinks you're 'troubled' and need understanding, which just pisses Mom off."

Shay stopped crunching. "You're kidding." Her pouty expression suddenly shifted. Her eyes brightened. Not the reaction I'd expected.

"Kenny's worried about me? Really?" A smile lit her face, and her eyes narrowed thoughtfully. "That's very interesting."

"Yeah, what's so great about that?"

She didn't answer but bounded into the bathroom, shutting the door behind her. Then I heard the shower going full blast.

Weird. But I was too hyped about talking to Nick to worry about my sister.

You're probably wondering why I didn't just break down and confide in Shay about the Nick stuff, considering her expertise with men. Well, first, it would be too gross to have my family in my business (of course Shay would tell Angela everything), and second, Shay was way too absorbed in the Kenny and Angela drama to be bothered.

Time to handle my own business. I had plans, and they went like this:

Hunt down Nick. Break the news to him and say goodbye to any future hookups between us. Then tell

CJ and Tash everything so we could move on and be the Terrible Three once again.

Message BoaRD

You know, even though they laughed at first, I bet CJ and Tasha ended up feeling terrible about what happened at the Happy Buddha. I bet after they thought things over, they really wanted to talk to Genesis seriously. I bet they were as worried as she was about the whole thing.

CJ and Tasha should have remembered that Genesis was the ONLY girl in the universe who would be friends with them. Seriously! they will never ever find another girl who will want to hang out with them. no matter what happened with nick, they should have been damned grateful for genesis!

MOST RECENT ENTRIES   CALENDAR

VIEW FRIENDS   LINKS   PHOTOS

07/04 06:34:36

CONFESSIONS OF A BOYFRIEND STEALER— BLOG BY GENESIS BELL

[10TH ENTRY]

Oh, yeah. They were so grateful. Wait till you read the stupid text message I got from CJ the morning after the Happy Buddha incident. It said:

hooking up with nick tonight? ROTFL . . . cj PS. HA, HA, HA!

I wanted to smash my Palm Pilot. Obviously, she and Tasha still thought I was a huge joke. I couldn't stand it.

Aside from that asinine IM, I hadn't heard from her or Tasha since the Happy Buddha. I knew they were waiting for me to apologize, since I was the one who'd stormed out of the restaurant. Terribles are supposed to be cool, after all. If you blew it, you had to make amends.

One more day and holiday break would be over,

and then I'd face them in person. Despite how irritating CJ was, I had to suck it up and fix our friendship.

It was just that I had to talk to Nick first, in person. He deserved that much, after all we'd been through together. Crap, I was nervous. I was afraid I'd still be into him. I was afraid he'd want to kiss me when we really had to be platonic buddies from now on. I was afraid he'd freak when I told him that I was confessing everything to CJ.

But it was time to get a grip, so I called Nick's house. His mom told me he was working at the greenhouse until dinnertime.

"I'm sure Nick would be thrilled to have some company," she told me. "Working at the greenhouse can be a little boring." She giggled. "I know. His dad drags me down there every so often."

Amazingly, she gave me directions to the greenhouse without even asking my name. I thought most normal parents were more paranoid these days. But what did I know about normal parents?

As I drove, I reminded myself that at least this trauma-drama would be over soon. CJ and Tash would be mad at me once they realized Nick and I had really made out, but they'd get over it because of Fiesta Beach. After all, my documentary might get on MTV. Both of them are deadly serious about being rich and famous someday.

Tasha's big goal is to be a weather reporter on the Weather Channel. She's decided that she could easily dominate the entire channel, since she's better-looking and more charismatic than anyone they have on there now. She wants to become a well-known media personality, sort of the Vanna White of Doppler radar. Tasha and I are both average students (except I get A's in media class). Tasha's parents baby her, though, and always blame the school instead of Tasha.

CJ always gets A's, though she never cracks a book. She's so lucky; she is supposed to be gifted or a genius. CJ expects to waltz into some Ivy League school after graduation. She's researched which ones have the highest number of the richest kids in America and figures she'll either become a trophy wife or fall into some money-making venture where someone else does all the work. She fully expects to become a billionaire one way or another.

Knowing CJ and Tasha the way I do, I'm sure they'll get exactly what they want. But that's way, way into the future, and my documentary was now, which gave me an edge. I was just fantasizing about making my way to Toronto or New York or L.A. when the Pilateses' greenhouse sprang into view. It's nothing much to look at, just a long, squat, steamy-windowed building next to a little blocky office building. A few stubby pines surrounded the place.

All I knew was that Nick Pilates was somewhere nearby.

My already racing heart was just about bursting out of my chest. I hadn't seen him in days, not since Leaden.

I parked my mom's Mustang in the gravel lot and

immediately spotted Nick leaning against the main office building, smoking. Busted! He was supposed to have quit months ago. CJ would have been furious. I guess it was her right to be pissed since she was the girlfriend. Girlfriends are allowed to rule over a guy's health, looks, manners, and money, or so Shay and Angela say.

I didn't know what I was supposed to do. As the unclassified girl in his life, I decided I should play it cool.

He saw me before I could call out hello. Nick stomped the cigarette out with his heel.

"Gen, hey," he said, and then grinned. "You here to buy some plants?" He gestured to the greenhouse. Some customers were coming out carrying an assortment of lush green plants and small trees.

"Not hardly." I stared at the cigarette on the ground. I thought I should say something. Kissing him gave me some jurisdiction, right? "I thought you gave them up."

He shrugged. "I did, and I will again." He ran his fingers through his hair. "It's no big deal."

"Oh, yeah, I guess," I said lamely.

"So—" Nick stopped and suddenly looked over his shoulder. He was really squinting hard at the office building behind us.

I wanted to say, "Hello, I'm standing right here in front of you."

"What's up?" he mumbled, suddenly finishing his sentence.

He was still looking over his shoulder.

"Maybe I shouldn't have stopped by. Maybe you're busy." I was getting a little pissed. Weren't we at least friends? Did he even remember that we'd kissed?

Finally, he turned around.

"It's not that. It's just that I can't talk too long or my old man will be out here going nuts. He hates it when I take too many breaks." Nick grimaced, looking over his shoulder again.

Somebody suddenly started talking in a really loud voice, and it was coming from the office building. I bet it was Nick's dad, because Nick started fidgeting even more. I realized he was going to bolt soon. It was time to shoot. "I've been talking to CJ and she thinks you've been seeing Sherryn Feldman while she was away."

Nick froze. "Uh, she does?"

"I have to tell her the truth."

Nick suddenly stared at the ground. "Yeah . . . well . . . uh . . ."

"Anyway, I just wanted to let you know," I said. "It's only fair."

Nick still stared at the ground. He wasn't saying a word.

I nudged his foot with mine. "Hello? Are you paying attention? I'm gonna tell CJ you were with *me,* not with Sherryn."

He was still staring at the ground.

"I can't let Sherryn take the rap. Not when she was totally innocent—"

His face was turning red now.

It hit me. Omigod. Omigod! Hello? How dense was I?

I took a step back. "I can't believe you!"

"Listen, Gen, it was only once. I didn't even plan it. Sherryn stopped by and we . . ." Nick gave me this helpless, little-boy look.

I so wanted to kick his ass. And to think that I had actually defended Sherryn, that skank, to CJ and Tasha! Omigod.

"Listen, Gen . . ."

"You are the biggest jerk on the planet!"

Now I really wanted to smack him.

Nick caught my hand. "Don't be mad, Gen. Sherryn is nice and everything, but I'm not into her."

"Omigod. I still can't believe you were really with Sherryn—" I yanked my hand free.

"It was a total mistake, Gen. You know I like you."

Man, I should have known Nick was a player. "What about CJ?"

"We're not like some married couple."

I couldn't believe it. I couldn't believe the crap that was coming out of Nick's mouth. And to think I thought he was sexy and sweet, and to think I was worried that it would be difficult to go totally platonic!

"So, you and me, we're friends, right?" Nick was babbling, trying to look into my eyes. "So let's just keep this quiet, okay?"

Friends? I don't think so.

I know. I know how it sounds. I'd made out with my best friend's guy and was pissed that he'd made out with someone else too. How hypocritical. But I didn't care at that point.

"CJ is my best friend. I have to tell her everything."

"That is a totally bad idea."

I looked him in the eye. "Lies can really hurt a relationship."

Nick shook his head. "Forget it." He looked at the squashed cigarette on the ground as if he wanted to snatch it back up. "Let me tell you—lies can really *help* a relationship. No one wants to hear the truth."

I wanted to scream. Nick had cheated on me with Sherryn. Or who knows? Maybe he'd cheated on Sherryn with me. I didn't even know who he saw first. Like it mattered.

Now what was I going to tell CJ and Tash? This was totally humiliating.

"I've got to go, okay? The old man will be out here any minute." He started to walk away and then stopped to look back at me. "I really had fun with you, Gen. You're a cool girl."

Like I was going to believe that. Maybe Nick and I really made a good pair. He was a two-faced player, and I was a boyfriend stealer.

He was stepping into the office building just as this big, balding, scowling guy came barreling out. He and Nick said a few words, and Nick nodded quickly, so I guessed that was his dad. Then they both went inside.

My nose was running, and the wind blew my hair around. The sun went behind the clouds, as if to say, No way am I going to shine on you and make you look good.

I decided to take the shortcut home, since my mother would go ballistic if I didn't get her precious Mustang back before dark. I drove fast. I was dangerous. I tossed my bangs out of my eyes. I was one of those chicks who leap around, throw punches, and kick midair, à la *The Matrix*.

The Mustang was okay, but it's not fierce enough for me. Someday, I'll have my own car. I have my eye on a Porsche or a Dodge Viper. I know everyone wants a hot car, but I'm really going to get one. If anyone deserved it, I did, I thought, especially after all I'd been through with Nick and CJ and Tasha and Sherryn Feldman. I needed something . . .

Suddenly, I realized that I could use my show for something good. My theme could be powerful and important. I could tell the audience firsthand how friends and lovers messed each other around. Tell them all about betrayal and stuff. I sure was an expert by that point. Not to mention being an expert on feeling totally stupid and idiotic.

I could do that, but would I want to? Fiesta Beach was supposed to be totally raw and unscripted. I sighed. I figured I'd just tape it as I saw it. No manipulations.

But back to reality. I had to tell the Terribles the truth, even though it meant maximum embarrassment. I couldn't afford more lies; my friendship with CJ and Tasha was at stake, and besides, it was bound to come out about Sherryn anyway. One of Sherryn's friends would end up blabbing.

My situation just went from crap (betraying CJ) to supercrap (being humiliated by Nick). God, this would happen to Jan Brady if she was on the WB or even Fox today. This was so nighttime soap opera! I wanted to hurl.

I snuck into my house, hoping I could make it to my bedroom before my sister or mother saw me, just in case either happened to be home. The living room was empty. Yes! I was halfway down the hall when my mother ambushed me from the kitchen.

She was super dressed-up, classy, and not at all hoochie-mama. Her hair was in a French twist, and she was wearing an expensive skirt and jacket, probably from Nordstrom or Bebe. She was wearing her hundred-and-twenty-three-dollar-a-bottle perfume. She was also gripping an unlit cigarette.

"Where have you been? I hope you parked the Mustang in the driveway. Kenny was supposed to be here thirty minutes ago."

I didn't really see what one thing had to do with the other, but my mother didn't have to make sense.

"You didn't see Kenny's car coming this way, did you?"

"Sorry," I said. "What's the big deal, anyway? He's probably stuck in traffic. They're doing construction all over the place."

My stomach grumbled. I was so hungry (from stress, I'm sure), but I knew that if I wanted to eat soon I'd better calm my mother down or I'd end up in a really long conversation that would result in my collapsing from starvation. Especially if Kenny was delayed or not coming at all, God forbid.

"Kenny's always on time, and he always calls if he's going to be even five minutes late." She was frowning anxiously. She began to pace and wave her unlit cigarette in the air. "I just need to hear from—"

Like magic, our phone rang. My mother gasped. "You get it!"

I ran, not bothering to ask her why. It was Kenny. Hallelujah, Lord.

"Um, Genesis, is your mother there?" His voice sounded odd. "I have to apologize to her for being so tardy. . . ." Yeah, he really used the word *tardy*.

I held the phone closer, since his voice was so soft. "She's really freaked out. Is something wrong?" I know it was nosy of me to ask, but I was curious.

"Something . . . unexpected . . . I really can't explain." He stammered. "I'll have to make it up to your mother. I hope she'll forgive me."

My mother grabbed the phone from me before I could say anything else, even goodbye.

I was a little curious about Kenny, but not enough to stick around. Besides, Angela could handle the situation. She was the pro, not me. I hurried into my bedroom. I so needed a break after all I'd been through.

I swear I was feeling faint from hunger. If only Kenny would come and get Angela; then I could relax enough to stuff my face. It would be so wonderful to veg out and forget about my life for a while. But if Angela saw me preparing food while she was in the middle of a drama, I'd never hear the end of it.

Yippee! I heard the front door shut and then a car start up. Guess my mom and Kenny were on their way, finally. I could eat first and build up my strength, which was what I'd need to focus on the Tasha, CJ, and Nick situation.

I searched the freezer for something good. I love waffles, and we even had frozen yogurt to go on top. Later I'd have to take care of the stack of bills in the kitchen. God forbid Angela should get cut off from Nordstrom or Saks. Plus, I really didn't want to lose my cable.

The phone rang and I ran to check Caller ID. I'd been avoiding e-mails, phone calls, and my PDA all day.

It was Chi. I hesitated. Did I really want to hear him whine and moan about Tasha? Not that she would care. Tasha was so confident that she thought it was great when Chi cried on my shoulder. It meant she didn't have to listen to him.

Chi was so cute, so rich, and usually such a funny, great guy, but Tasha had turned him into wimpy pulp. It was gross. On the other hand, Chi has always treated me really nice. After dealing with Nick, I deserved a little TLC. Maybe Chi would build up my confidence so I could tackle the Terribles. At least listening to his troubles would help me forget mine for a while.

Thirty minutes later, I'd agreed to meet Chi at the International House of Pancakes (www.ihop.com) to discuss Tasha. He was really upset because she'd been avoiding him all weekend. Typical Tasha. She took Chi's money and left him high and dry.

The bills would have to wait. IHOP waffles beat frozen every time. Best of all, Chi was treating, but it wasn't a date. It was just a counseling session.

Message Board

✉ I'M BACK AND I'M GLAD I DIDN'T MISS THIS PART — queenSheba — at 11:34 P.M.
I couldn't get online for a while, so I just got caught up with Gen's blog. I was SO disappointed in Nick. What a creep. What a slut-boy. Poor Gen. I know I've been harsh on her, but she made big mistakes. I think people should be responsible and righteous. Gen must have felt like dirt, though, finding out Nick played her and CJ both. God, I'd have wanted to just die.

✉ Re: I'M BACK AND I'M GLAD I DIDN'T MISS THIS PART — 007ugo — at 11:40 P.M.
Yeah, I agree, queenSheba. guess those playah rumors were true. ☹ Poor Gen. I think it's good she decided to meet Chi. I've talked to Chi once and he's a real sweetie.

That is such a bummer about Nick. Poor, poor Gen. Why do guys act like that? I wonder if that Sherryn ever found out the truth about Nick. Chi sounds awesome. I'm glad Gen had Chi, since she wasn't able to talk to CJ or Tasha.

I've seen Sherryn in action, and she is a total flirt. She wouldn't care about Nick. I know I don't listen to gossip, but I know someone who knows Sherryn really well.

i just hope Gen agreed to meet Chi for the right reasons. you know, she might have been looking for romance, after being dissed by Nick. i think girls can get into bad habits, like once you steal one friend's man you might find it easy to steal another one!

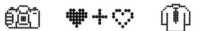

08/04 09:45:11

CONFESSIONS OF A BOYFRIEND STEALER— BLOG BY GENESIS BELL

[11TH ENTRY]

Listen, after my Nick encounter, I was totally immune to romance. I was totally focused on my documentary and my television career. Really. But despite that, I could still appreciate Chi's (many) wonderful qualities—in an objective way, of course.

← →

First, let me tell you just how adorable Chi is. He dresses like no other guy at school. Really cool, but not so fashionable that he looks like some geeky model or some poser weirdo. He also has these high cheekbones, long lashes, and great hair, and is tall with a nice swimmer's body. He's the top diver on our school's team, by the way.

Some friend of my mom's once said that Asian men just don't do it for her because they're all short

128

and skinny, which shows how stupid and racist many people are. All girls check Chi out, and lots would love to go out with him. Too bad he's too obsessed with Tasha to notice.

He was already seated at a booth in IHOP and waved when he saw me. He was way back in a dark corner, and as usual, his face was gloomy. The restaurant was crowded, mostly with kids, but I didn't see anyone I knew. There are three other high schools in the area, and everyone likes hanging out at IHOP.

It was pretty noisy in there. People were laughing and talking and a few were screaming at the top of their lungs. For some reason, you put some kids in a restaurant and they act like babies at Disney. They practically scream the whole time, throw food, and jump around in their seats like idiots.

I made my way to Chi's table and barely avoided sliding on some hash browns someone had just thrown on the floor.

Chi's situation with Tash was pathetic, and it had been going on for six months. She made him so nuts that most of his guy friends had long since refused to talk with him about her. They told him he was whipped, crazy, a dumbass, and that he needed Prozac or something stronger.

"Hi, Genesis," he said in a dark, brooding voice. "Thanks for meeting me like this. You're the only who understands. I feel so messed up these days. . . ."

"No prob," I said. "I'm just glad to be getting out of

the house. You have no idea how glad." I rolled my eyes and made a dramatic face, hoping for a smile from him, but no luck.

Chi just sighed. "I'll call the waitress over. I know you're hungry." He was sipping black coffee. Of course. He was even wearing black.

"What about you? I'll feel stupid eating by myself." How could anyone sit in IHOP and not pig out? That was the point. No one goes just to drink coffee—that's what Starbucks is for.

"I know I'm being a bummer," Chi said. "It's just that I can't stop thinking about Tash and worrying about our future together." He rubbed his eyes. "I've been too upset to eat," he went on. "Which isn't good for my diving. Coach says I've been looking pretty weak lately."

Emotional turmoil turns me into a turbo-eater. I usually don't stop until every crumb is gone. I'm lucky I have a fast metabolism. "Maybe food is just what you do need. Order *something*. You'll feel better, I promise."

Chi smiled a little. God, he was cute. "Okay, Mom. I'll get the silver-dollar pancakes."

"Just remember who's boss, sonny." I cackled and shook my finger at him. "Unless you want a time-out."

He laughed and shook his head. "I don't think anyone cheers me up like you do."

"That's sweet of you."

His smile disappeared. "Sweet. Maybe that's my problem, Gen. Maybe everyone thinks I'm this big marshmallow. Maybe that's why Tash treats me so bad."

The waitress took our order, poured Chi more coffee, and brought me an ice water.

I was glad for the interruption, because I really didn't know what to say. Chi was right about Tasha, but people in relationships don't like hearing the truth. Omigod, I sounded like Nick Pilates. I so did not want to go there.

"I don't understand Tasha at all," Chi continued after the waitress left. "She says I am way better than all of her old boyfriends, and that makes me feel great. But I never know where I stand with her. Maybe she's scared of getting hurt. . . ."

His eyes bored into mine. Man, was he intense, and man, was he wrong about Tasha. She wasn't fragile or fearful. She was a true Terrible, through and through. He should go back to that marshmallow theory, I thought.

"I'm just tired of feeling so miserable."

Chi paused and ran his hands through his hair, mussing it up (which made it even cuter). "I keep thinking we're getting closer, but then she blows me off again. Our relationship is just crazy. It's like everything's out of control."

Something made me lean forward and say, "Maybe she likes it crazy and out of control. Have you ever thought about how easily Tasha gets bored?"

He just stared at me.

"Think about it. If you guys were always happy, she'd lose it. She likes drama, and I don't think she's going to change. You want a relationship. She wants a soap opera."

I paused to catch my breath. Chi was in shock. His mouth had dropped open. I usually told him that of course Tasha loved him and that he just had to be patient, blah, blah.

"I know Tasha's really deep—"

The poor guy was in denial. Tasha was only deep about a few things in life, and they were expensive clothes, facials, skiing, and Tasha herself. (Yes, I'm being catty—but truthful.)

"So what should I do? Just give up on her?"

"I'm not saying that. Just stop trying to change her."

Chi stared down at the table. "I guess I have been pressuring her, haven't I? I didn't mean to, it's just . . . I don't know what else to do."

The waitress appeared then and plopped silver-dollar pancakes in front of Chi, Belgian waffles in front of me, and a bunch of syrups and a bowl of butters in the middle of the table.

I really wanted to eat but I had to answer him first. "You haven't done anything wrong, except . . ."

I paused to put butter on my waffle while it was still hot. If you wait too long, the butter doesn't melt, so it was really important that I act fast.

Chi hadn't touched his pancakes. "So, okay, what did I do wrong? And what should I do to make it right? If that's even possible . . ."

"Love Tasha enough to leave her alone."

His jaw dropped. "You mean break up with her?"

I shook my head. "Let *her* come to *you*. That's all I'm saying. Stop calling her. Stop IMing her. Stop e-mailing her. She'll get intrigued, trust me."

"She'll get pissed. She'll find another boyfriend," Chi said, but he didn't look so sure.

Let me just say that I really was trying to help. I know her like no one else. CJ doesn't count. The only way Chi was going to win with Tasha was to play it cool.

I'm sure people had told him this before. Maybe he was finally ready to listen. He suddenly seemed a little less intense.

He stared into space. "I could try it your way, but I don't know about playing games. . . ." He shook his head. "That's not really me. . . ."

He cut into his pancakes and started eating. I was happy, because I was so ready to *eat*. You know, the kind of eating when you don't come up for air for minutes? For a while, we were both too busy chowing down to do any more blabbing. It was great.

I looked up and found Chi staring at me. I squirmed. Maybe I had syrup on my face.

Chi said, "You know, sometimes I wonder if love is worth it. It shouldn't be so hard."

I nodded wisely as if I had a clue. I nonchalantly wiped my mouth with a napkin.

Chi was still staring at me, which was a little weird. But now he was smiling. I could feel myself blushing.

"I've driven everyone crazy about this Tasha stuff. It's like I've ruined my whole life over her." He reached across the table to squeeze my hand. "What would I do without you, Gen? You've saved me." I wanted to squeeze his hand back but thought that might give the wrong message. "Do you think we could get together again? Talking to you helps me think clearer."

Tasha wouldn't care. She and CJ loved it when I offered an ear to their lovesick guys. I was their buffer girl.

"Sure," I said. "That would be cool. Hey, I don't have anyone I can really open up to either." Which was true.

He was still holding my hand, but I didn't mind.

"I want you to know that I'm here for you too," he said. "You're not only a great friend, but you're beautiful too, inside and out."

Wow. I could feel my face heat up. No one's ever said anything like that to me before. He even sounded sincere.

"I mean it," Chi said, reading my mind. "I'm not bullshitting you. I think you're awesome."

Oh man. I suddenly realized there was no way I could ever tell Chi about what happened with Nick and me . . . and Sherryn. Chi would think I was a skank. He'd never compliment me again, especially not my insides.

He stared into my eyes. For a moment, neither of us said anything. It was kind of awkward but sweet too. Then he let go of my hand, which was too bad. He has really nice hands. Not clammy or cold.

"I'm finally getting it together, thanks to you." He took a big bite of pancake. "I'm tired of talking about my problems. How about telling me what's up with you?"

My documentary was the safest topic, and I was curious about what other people would think. Chi was other people, and he was supersmart; everyone said he'd end up being a lawyer or a doctor. I really respected his opinion on non-Tasha subjects. Besides, just hanging out with him was cheering me up. Maybe he'd tell me again how awesome and beautiful I was. I could hope.

Message Board

✉ **Danger, Danger!—queenSheba—at 3:30 P.M.**

genesis must have been blind. chi was really getting into her! chi is such a total cutie and so sweet. i don't know him but you can tell. it is obvious that poor chi was ready to fall for someone new after tasha had been so rotten to him. i think gen must have known what was going on. it almost seemed like she was encouraging him.

✉ **Re: Danger, Danger!—007ugo—at 4:12 P.M.**

You're so wrong, queenSheba. Chi ONLY needed a friend and Gen was there for him. Period. Anyway, if way, way down the road, they got together, I think that would be great. Gen deserves a really good guy in her life.

✉ Re: Danger, Danger!—JUICYFRUIT45—at 4:30 P.M.

I just wish I could meet someone like Chi. You wonder why he hooked up with Tasha in the first place. Do guys only look at pretty faces? I'm glad Genesis was there for him. I have to agree with queenSheba, though. I think Chi was a little attracted to Gen. Gen must have noticed.

MOST RECENT ENTRIES   CALENDAR
VIEW FRIENDS   LINKS   PHOTOS

09/04 08:32:26

CONFESSIONS OF A BOYFRIEND STEALER—
BLOG BY GENESIS BELL

[12TH ENTRY]

I guess you had to be there. Everything was very innocent between Chi and me. I would have known if he had been hitting on me (which he wasn't). We just made each other feel better. We were just helping each other out. I needed all the support I could get to face what was coming!

← →

Break was over, and it was back to the real world—school, that is, not the MTV show. For once I didn't mind going back to the smelly halls, the hideous cafeteria food, the crabbed-out teachers, and the endless stream of boring homework. I couldn't wait to start to work on my Fiesta Beach documentary. I was going to make TV history. But first, I really, really had to clear things up with CJ and Tash, even though revealing that

Nick had two-timed both CJ and me with Sherryn was going to be so rank.

But before I went through that ordeal, I decided I'd do something positive and proactive for my TV show. That meant tracking down Andy Fortis, who was holding Fiesta Beach at his house at the end of the month. Fortis is a senior, a big-time partier, and a member of the rich-kid clique. His parents take off for Europe every winter.

"A documentary?" he said. "Hey, that's awesome. Let's do it." He grinned. "But only if I get a DVD copy."

I held out my hand. "You got a deal."

He slapped my palm. "Just throw in some hot T and A shots, okay?"

I rolled my eyes. Right, filming other girls' body parts would do wonders for my reputation. Maybe if I were trying to establish myself as a high-profile lesbian.

This was going to be my show. Totally. Fortis said he'd be putting signs all over the house that basically said PARTY AND DOCUMENTARY FILMING INSIDE. ENTER AND BE TAPED.

I was relieved. I was trying to cover all the bases, like a true pro.

Tasha, CJ, and I all have first-hour study hall together, so it was time to face them. It was do or die time. The Terribles would rise above this, I knew, but I'd be the one who'd look like a total ass (considering the Nick/Sherryn angle). Crap, this was going to be so mortifying.

Tasha and CJ were waiting at our table, which was

in the back near the good window. We always sat there because we were the Terrible Three and it was just a given. Actually, CJ had claimed it from the beginning, and people were afraid to cross her.

They waved me over. It was pretty quiet, which is normal. Everyone's comatose first hour, especially in study hall, which is usually where everyone goofs off.

Tasha was touching up her nails; CJ was eating a bag of M&M's. CJ has this demented idea that only food you eat at meals has calories. So she starves herself at breakfast, lunch, and dinner and then sucks down handfuls of candy whenever she can. It is so dysfunctional, and yet she's a twig, barely a size two.

I slid into the chair and took several deep breaths.

The heaters in our room were clanking like crazy. I dug my nails into my palms.

CJ said the second I sat down, "So, what's this I hear about the local news wanting to cover your documentary?"

Before I could answer, Tasha jumped in. "Yeah, someone said Channel Seven is interested in using some clips for a special on teens. Is that true?"

"I just hope you use good lighting," CJ said. She scowled. "I refuse to look fat on camera because you don't know what you're doing."

I wished the gossips had waited until after study hall to start their crazy rumors.

"Wait, guys," I said. "Before you go there—"

"I mean it, Genesis." CJ shot me a dark look. "I've heard that the camera adds ten pounds anyway."

I plunged in, "Listen, we can discuss all that later, but first I have to tell you something important." I made myself look into CJ's eyes and then Tasha's, so they'd know I was serious. "*Super* important.

"I am really, really sorry, but Nick and I did hook up. I swear I didn't plan for it to happen. He only came over to watch *Scary Movie 2* with me, and then we—"

"Omigod, I can't believe you, Genesis," CJ interrupted in a low, mean voice. "I *thought* you were finally going to have the decency to apologize for that stupid stunt you pulled at the Happy Buddha." She glared at me ferociously. "I thought you were trying to keep Tasha and me from going after Sherryn, but now I think you're just twisted."

I gaped at her.

CJ continued. "You were *not* with Nick, period. I really, really resent you lying and pushing your delusions onto everyone."

"Just wait a second," I said. My heart was racing like crazy. I just wanted to make things right between us. I just wanted to fix things. "You have to listen to me—"

"Keep your voice down," CJ hissed. "Do you want people to hear?" She glanced around, but no one was looking our way. Most kids were asleep or sitting glassy-eyed with headphones on.

"You have to listen," I repeated more softly.

"No, I don't. You are totally not Nick's type, so just stop," CJ said. "You're starting to sound pathetic."

My face got hot. She hadn't just said that.

Tasha interrupted, looking flustered. "Guys, can't we all just get along?"

"You won't let me talk—" I choked out.

"Because it's crap," CJ hissed.

"Just cool it, Gen, okay?" Tasha nudged me. "You gotta get a grip—seriously. Let's just move on to something else."

"That's a good idea," CJ said. "As long as Gen stops this delusional stuff about Nick, we'll be fine." She glanced around the room. "Right, Gen?"

I couldn't answer. I just stared at her, but I guess she took that as a yes.

All I knew was that my stomach was twisting wildly, and my face felt like it was on fire. I couldn't believe CJ, one of my best friends, would treat me like this. I know, I know, I was the boyfriend stealer . . . but still . . . didn't they get it? What about Tasha, just blowing me off? They couldn't shut me out. I was a Terrible. They were treating me like a joke.

". . . so excited about being on TV!" Tasha was saying, as if nothing was wrong. "I wonder if anyone else will be videotaping the party."

I had to pull myself together. I clasped my hands. They were shaking, but just a little.

"First, I'm not just videotaping the party; I'm producing a *professional* hour-long documentary. Channel Seven isn't involved at all."

The Fiesta Beach documentary. That was what mattered. This was going to be my biggest moment ever. I was going to be a major television producer. I had to become famous now. It would so make up for this crap.

"I think it's going to be so cool. I'm getting a body wrap and a fake tan at one of those spray-on places," Tasha gushed.

"I don't see how it will be professional when you're just using a camcorder," CJ said.

"It will be professional because *I'm* professional." My voice didn't even wobble.

"You're going to be like the director, right?" Tasha was opening her makeup case and her compact.

"I'm going to produce and direct."

CJ and Tasha stared at me. Tasha was holding a mascara wand in the air.

"My show is going to be totally different from anyone else's." I ran my fingers through my hair. "It's going to be fresh and original."

CJ smirked. "You sound like *TV Guide.* So, is Nick going to be a part of your blockbuster?"

My hand ached to slap her, not that I've slapped anyone before. "Maybe."

"CJ and I will be part of it, right?" Tasha looked at me eagerly.

Oh yeah, they'd be in it all right. Evil visions of taping unflattering angles of CJ floated through my head. "I wouldn't leave you guys out." I wasn't sure how I meant that at the time.

"Get shots of me and Chi. He's photogenic, and we look awesome together." Tasha was pulling out more makeup.

"And take some of Nick and me—*together*," CJ said snidely.

My hand itched again.

"It's going to be awesome," Tasha said, opening her blush tube.

"Whatever." CJ was wearing one of her famous pouts.

CJ and Tasha then started talking about a new nail place that has great acrylic tips and a salon that offers this expensive Japanese thermal perm. I mentioned that I met Chi at IHOP; Tasha didn't bother responding (poor Chi). By that point, Tasha and CJ were too busy talking about a new herbal diet drink that makes you skinny but also gives you the runs.

At least they had their priorities straight.

MESSAGE BOARD

✉ **FRIENDS?**—JUICYFRUIT45—AT 9:46 P.M.
I can't believe how Tasha and CJ treated Gen. They wouldn't even listen to her story! I don't know why. Maybe they were too into themselves to care about other people's lives. I hope I never meet CJ and Tasha!

✉ **Re: FRIENDS?**—007UGO—AT 11:35 P.M.
Tasha and CJ couldn't handle the truth (didn't Jack Nicholson say that in a movie?). CJ and Tasha wouldn't listen to Genesis because then they would have had to realize that they DON'T rule the world!!! CJ and Tasha always thought all guys belonged to

them, and they couldn't stand to hear that this wasn't true!

✉ Re: FRIENDS?—QUEENSHEBA—AT 12:12 A.M.
i'd be so upset. having your friends mad at you can turn your world into a huge mess. i don't know if i could cope if that happened to me.

10/04 08:13:39

Confessions of a Boyfriend Stealer—
Blog by Genesis Bell

[13th entry]

I did cope, because I was tough. After all, I'd been raised in the Bell household (which is a good place to learn some jungle skills). I wasn't even tempted to quit school and run away. I had a lot to do.

← →

It was already Friday, and we were two weeks into the new semester. That meant Fiesta Beach was only fourteen days away. God. I couldn't believe I was really producing my own television show. I'd been trying to learn how to use all the advanced features on my Sony. My camcorder had some really cool features. I could make everything move in slow motion, or make things look artistically out of focus, or re-create the jerky camera motions à la *Blair Witch*. There was tons of stuff I still hadn't tried, but I was pushing hard. It wasn't easy, though, and I was practicing as much as possible. *Alien Love* had been really simple in comparison.

I barely saw the Terribles, which was really a good thing. I couldn't deal with them.

I had so much on my mind that for once the silent war going on between Angela and Shay didn't bother me too much. I knew they'd explode eventually, but I hoped it would wait until after I'd made my show.

Of course, all my teachers were piling on the homework as usual. They didn't realize that Fiesta Beach had to be my top priority. They didn't realize I might be making television history.

I was still toying with different themes, and I knew I had to latch onto something quickly. One idea was to make it a dark documentary. Maybe I'd show how emotionally exhausting it was to be a part of high school society. Let's face it, most TV shows and movies about teens are bogus. No matter what the theme was, my Fiesta Beach show was going to be the real deal. Maybe I'd show the down and dirty side. Maybe my documentary would be revealing. Really revealing . . .

Maybe CJ, Tash, and Nick had better watch their asses. I grinned. It was very therapeutic to fantasize about filming certain people so that their asses looked huge and their pores looked even huger. But I'd keep it all professional. No one was going to ruin this for me.

I was realizing, however, that I was *superpissed* at CJ and Tasha. I was also getting a clue about Miss Anorexica. If she'd really thought I was a big joke, she wouldn't have been so nasty when I tried to confess about Nick. No, that wasn't it. The problem was that she knew I was telling her the truth, and it was killing her that a Jan Brady type like me could steal her man. I also knew that she'd never admit anything. As for Tasha, she'd go along with CJ, as usual. As *always.*

The more I figured the Terribles out, the madder I got, but then I'd think about my hookup with Nick and feel guilty, and then I couldn't stand thinking about any of it, period. I was so glad I had Fiesta Beach to distract me.

Luckily, my documentary debut was stirring up a lot of excitement and interest. It seems like everyone wants to be a producer or an assistant these days. Kids were stopping me in the hallway and in class with all kinds of opinions about what my show should be like. (Some I'd already thought of and some were too dumb or crazy for words. One guy wanted a wet T-shirt contest and some girl wanted to include a talent show.) It was a shock that people noticed me without CJ and Tasha at my side.

On top of everything, I had to deal with Nick. Ever since I'd blown him off at the greenhouse, he'd been IMing, e-mailing, and calling me like crazy. He claimed he wanted us to be friends. Right. Nick was totally cocky. He was so sure he could play me, CJ, Sherryn, and any other girl—and get away with it all. He obviously couldn't handle the fact that I was over him. I didn't answer any of his messages.

Chi and I were IMing back and forth a lot, but just

as friends. He was really sweet, and it was all very innocent. I swear. I learned my lesson. Chi was just being supportive about Fiesta Beach, and that was it.

I did notice that Chi didn't mention Tasha at all. Instead, he talked a lot about how his diving was improving. He'd asked me if I wanted to come watch him practice. I was vague and told him I would someday. I'd love to check out Chi in his Speedo, but I didn't want to give the wrong message by acting like I was into him. I had enough trouble already.

Friday of our first week back was almost over, and I was late for trig. Not that I was in a hurry. I'm not a big math fan, and besides, the weekend was almost here. That meant freedom . . . I wish. I had loads of homework, and I really needed to do more practice shots with the camcorder. What if I filmed everything in black-and-white? What if I could finally figure out how to use that fish-eye lens? At least my soft-focus shots were working.

I drifted down the hall in a fog. Life was too tiring these days. What I would have loved to do was just veg out and watch movies and forget all about reality. . . .

I screeched to a halt. Someone was standing right in front of me.

"Hey, Gen," Nick said, giving me his sexiest smile.

Damn. I hadn't seen him lurking nearby. Somehow, he'd timed it so that we'd meet when no one else was around. The halls were empty. Nick was the slickest dude on the planet.

"The second bell's about to ring," I said. "I've got to go." In other words, leave me alone.

He grabbed my arm and whispered in my ear, "C'mon, I've got something for you. You'll like it, I promise."

Before I could protest, he pulled me down a side corridor. I wanted to split, but I admit I was curious.

I noticed that he had one hand behind his back. He smiled his cute, sneaky, player smile. "I know you've been pissed at me, Gen, but I'll make it up to you, if you give me the chance." He thrust a long-stemmed red rose into my hand.

Okay, it was nice, even if my Angela-trained eyes told me this was a gas station rose. (You've seen them sold in cellophane at the cash register, right?) Nick was wacked if he thought that would make up for Sherryn.

"I really like you, Gen, and I just wish you'd let me prove it to you."

He was leaning down, and I realized his lips were only inches away from mine. He was going for a kiss—while CJ was somewhere in the very same building. I ducked and quickly stepped away. No way were those player lips locking onto mine.

"I thought we could talk," he said, trying to look intense and serious.

"We can't if we've got our tongues down each other's throats," I said. "Besides, what would we talk about? You and CJ, or you and Sherryn?"

"Listen, Sherryn and I aren't even seeing each

other, and CJ—well, man, I don't know what's up with her."

I couldn't believe him. I mean, yes, he and CJ probably were on shaky ground. I could tell CJ was in one of her restless stages. I'd heard her gushing over some new guy she'd met but wouldn't name. Of course, she wouldn't break up with Nick until she snared a good replacement boyfriend. She and Nick were still together, officially.

"Why can't you give me a break, Gen? I'm not trying to hurt you or anything. All I want is to be friends." Before I could stop him, he was pulling me close.

He was trying for a kiss—again! I pushed him away. I guess Nick thought being friends meant swapping spit.

I admit that not long before that I'd have been tempted, but finding out about Sherryn put a stop to those feelings—and to the guilt. Lucky I was well taught by Angela. I remembered two things: 1) Men who cheat on you once will do it again, and 2) Reject a player and he'll chase you like crazy. (Conversely, fall for a player and he'll run like crazy.)

Nick pouted. "I think we'd be really good together."

"The problem is"—I said snippily—"that I'm not into foursomes, Nick. I doubt Sherryn and CJ are either."

Nick went from sweet to sour in seconds. "I'm seeing a whole new side of you, Gen. You'd better watch out. Guys don't like harsh girls."

Like I was supposed to care what he thought. "Oh

well, that's their loss, then." I turned down a hall and left him standing there. "Later."

"Hey," he called out. "You got my rose."

"Yeah, I know."

It felt good to walk away, trust me.

But I was not surprised to hear Nick call out, "Hey, you'll change your mind, Gen!"

Yelling back "In your dreams" would have been too clichéd.

← →

It was Friday night, and it looked like I was going to spend it alone. I didn't mind at all. I wandered into the kitchen and stuck Nick's rose in a glass. It was pretty puny compared to the mammoth bouquets Shay and Angela usually got. But oh well. At least it was mine. I deserved something for all my troubles. I grabbed some M&M's and Doritos and headed for the living room. I really needed some downtime.

CJ was out with Nick. Maybe I *should* have told her about Nick giving me a rose and chasing me so hard, but I know CJ. She'd probably just call me mentally ill again. Tash was out with Chi (I guess she had nothing better to do). Shay was with one of her regular guys, and Angela was with Kenny. I was thrilled to have some peace and quiet.

I'd deal with my other homework tomorrow. I stretched out on the couch and was all settled to watch reruns of a documentary about beauty pageants (it brought back gross childhood memories) when the phone rang.

"Gen, you busy? Am I interrupting anything?" It was Chi, sounding a little nervous.

I sat up. "What's going on?"

"Tasha broke our date tonight." He took a deep breath. "I know she's gone out with some other guy—"

"I'm sorry, Chi," I said, and I really was. He deserved better.

"It's okay, but I thought we could meet at Denny's and talk."

"It's *okay*? Are you sure?"

I was shocked.

"Listen, I'll explain later. I'm buying. We could have some shakes and greasy fries and onion rings." He cleared his throat. "I can't wait to see you."

I told myself that this wasn't a date with yet another friend's boyfriend. Chi and I were really buds. I had to be there for him, so I agreed to rush over to Denny's.

But still, I decided Chi deserved a more beautiful me, so I threw on a really nice black top, put on a little makeup, and ran some mousse through my hair. I was about to raid my mother's perfume stash when I heard a noise in the living room.

I froze. Burglars, I thought, or maybe a serial killer. Then I heard the TV. Would a thief watch TV? I strained my ears to listen. It was a rerun of *The Golden Girls*.

Maybe it was an elderly burglar. I tiptoed down the hall, trying to remember if we had anything like a weapon around. Maybe my sister's Abdomenizer, which was pretty heavy. If I could hoist it up, I could knock the burglar out.

I held my breath and peered into the living room. Shay was sitting on the couch reading. I was so shocked that I let out a squeak. Shay was supposed to be out with one of her regulars, Justin or EJ. I couldn't remember which. That usually meant she wouldn't be home until morning. Plus, the shock of seeing Shay with a book nearly made me pass out.

"Shay?" I had to make sure it was really her and not some spooky alien double.

Shay let out a little scream and clutched the book to her chest.

"What are you doing here?" she demanded, in typical Shay attack mode.

I gave her the standard reply. "I live here."

I couldn't believe it. Shay was blushing! I didn't know she was biologically capable of it. Same for reading, come to think of it.

I was dying to know what she was reading. I tried to imagine why she was acting so bizarre and un-Shay-like. Was she reading porn? Nah, Shay wouldn't be embarrassed over that. So what was it?

I took a closer look and caught a glimpse of the title. I couldn't believe it. She was reading the Bible. The Bible, as in "Let there be light" and the flood and Jonah and that crowd.

I couldn't help it. I started laughing. Shay's face went from red to purple. She jumped to her feet.

"What's going on?" I tried to read her face, but she was looking away.

"None of your business, okay? Just leave me the hell alone!"

Wow, now I knew she was up to something weird. "Let me guess, Mom got herself a Jesus guy, and now you want one. It's just like when Mom got collagen in her lips, you had to get it too. Even though your lips are like completely big on their own."

She glared at me. "Just shut up, Genesis."

Who wouldn't ask questions if they caught Shay Bell, Miss Don't Bug Me About God and Crap, reading the Bible? "Am I right? I am! I know it!"

Clutching her Bible, she stormed out of the living room. I could have followed her and nagged her for answers, but that goes against the Bell household code: don't stick your nose in, and don't stick around when things get messy (unless they get *really* messy, and that means old bouncer Genesis has to smooth things over).

Shay wouldn't do anything truly bad; she knows better. I pushed away the uneasy feeling in my stomach. Angela thought she was in love, which was serious. No one would mess with that. It wasn't a spoken Bell household code, but I was sure we all got it. Shay might throw tantrums until she broke them up or quote the Bible to make them feel guilty about dating while Kenny was still legally married, but she wouldn't take it any further. She wouldn't.

Anyway, Chi was waiting, and I needed perfume. I

headed back to my mom's room and overheard Shay on the phone. I told you she has this deep, booming voice, and she doesn't know the meaning of the word *whisper.*

"—tomorrow morning? I really need to talk. Okay?"

I figured it was Justin or EJ offering a sympathetic shoulder for her to boo-hoo on, so I didn't bother listening anymore. Shay and dramatic phone conversations were boringly predictable. I sprayed myself with a little perfume, grabbed Shay's really cute suede jacket since it was so cold out, and split. Chi and Denny's (www.dennys.com) fries and onion rings were waiting.

MESSAGE BOARD

✉ ROSES—007UGO—AT 12:22 P.M.
It was ROMANTIC when Nick gave Genesis the rose. Genesis must have realized she had it going on and that she wasn't just the girl in the background anymore. Because even though he is a jerk, Nick is so gorgeous.

✉ RE: ROSES—JUICYFRUIT45—AT 12:34 P.M.
I have never had a guy give me a rose. I think it's a little cute that Nick gave one to Gen, even though he IS a jerk. I'm glad though that genesis got to be friends with chi. It must have been hard not to have her girlfriends around anymore. Tasha and cj are not nice, but they were almost like sisters to Gen.

✉ Re: Roses—QueenSheba—at 12:55 a.m.

i'm glad someone is paying attention to the issue of friendships. tasha and Cj looked out for genesis for a long time. i hope she didn't just decide to blow that off. i hope she didn't let the rose go to her head.

CONFESSIONS OF A BOYFRIEND STEALER— BLOG BY GENESIS BELL

[14TH ENTRY]

Maybe it looked like I was on top of the world. Like I was supercasual about the blowout with the Terribles and superbig-headed about Nick, but that wasn't the case at all. Dealing with my documentary, my family, my social life, and everything else totally stressed me out. I've gotten used to acting nonchalant in the middle of a disaster (which helped me survive growing up in the Bell household).

Chi was a real friend, which meant more to me than a gas station rose or even the expensive designer roses Angela and Shay always get.

← →

I walked into Denny's and immediately felt happy. First of all, Chi looked so cute. (I know I keep saying that, but it's true!) He wasn't as stylish as he usually is. His hair was a little messed up, and he was in jeans and a hoodie. Somehow, it made him seem more romantic.

He didn't look all sad and depressed for a change. He gave me a big smile and motioned for me to sit beside him in the booth. Wasn't that a little weird and a little cozy? But I sat there anyway because I didn't want him to feel rejected.

He was chowing down on fries and pushed the plate toward me. Amazing. He was a totally different guy from our last pig-out meeting.

"I know what you like, girl. Dig in." He popped a fry into my mouth.

Chi is usually such a broody guy. He was so upbeat he almost scared me.

I was too flabbergasted to say anything, but that was okay because Chi was chattering away a mile a minute.

"See, the thing is, Gen, that I've had this epiphany. I realized I had to get on with my life."

"Tasha—" I started to say.

"Look, I'll always love Tasha, but I know she's out there hooking up with other guys. I can't stop her and I can't hold on to her." He grinned at me.

"And that makes you . . . happy?" I was baffled. Could Chi be on 'shrooms or something?

"No, but I've got to stop living like a monk, you know? Maybe Tash and me are supposed to be free agents."

"Sure," I said. Like I had a clue.

The waitress bustled over and brought us Cokes and more fries. We dove in. Chi turned to stare at me intently.

"So, Gen, what's the story?"

I figured he wanted to hear how I was handling the stress over the Fiesta Beach show, but I had a mouth full of fries and couldn't answer right away.

Then Chi said, "I hear Nick Pilates is hot for you."

I nearly choked, and had to take a long drink of Coke.

"What? How? Who told you that?" I wanted to scream. This couldn't be happening. Nick was my dirty little secret.

"Nick told me you guys dated for a while. He still likes you." Chi frowned a little. "You deserve better than him, Gen. He's kind of a jerk. He's playing you and CJ both."

I buried my face in my hands. "Omigod. Nick was a huge mistake. I am *so* not dating him, I promise."

"Listen, I'm not judging you or anything. I was just curious—"

I wanted to hurl up my fries. I couldn't believe Nick was shooting off his mouth. I thought he didn't want CJ to know about our hookup. But of course, guys wouldn't rat him out to CJ. It was some male code.

"Nick and I kissed once—by accident," I managed to tell Chi, peeking at him through my fingers. "It was totally creepy of me, and I know it. I even told CJ about it. It is history, trust me." So I wasn't spilling the whole story.

Chi put his arm around me. "It's not a big deal. Nick and I have gym class together. He overheard me talking to Scott Wylie about your documentary."

"Omigod, then what?"

"Well, he said that you and he were tight. That you guys had first hooked up over break . . ."

I pulled my hands from my face. "I've told Nick that we're totally over. He's dating my best friend, for one thing. He's not my type, for another." Nick had briefly been my type, I admit it, but I wasn't going to tell Chi that.

Chi hugged me. "It's cool, Gen. I know you, and you're a good person. I just wanted to make sure that you weren't still into Pilates."

I grabbed my Coke and took a long drink.

"Well, I'm not."

"I'm glad to hear that," he said. "Listen, it's obvious that Tash and I aren't meant to be. We'll probably break up soon."

"Uh" was my only response. "Uh, I'm sorry."

Chi paused and gave me a shy smile.

"Don't be, Gen, because I was hoping I might have a chance with you."

Message Board

✉ I WaS RIGHT!—QueenSHeba—aT 6:34 a.m.

i think genesis planned to get chi the whole time. he

was upset over tasha. i've seen girls trap guys like that, by playing all sweet and nice. i bet you anything genesis and chi hooked up. chi deserves a great girlfriend!

✉ <u>Re: I WaS RIGHT!</u>—JUICYFRUIT45—aT 7:09 a.M.

Maybe Genesis and Chi did hook up, but maybe they decided they were falling in love. Genesis was a good friend to Chi. She listened to his problems when no one else would. So you really have to admit she would be a good girlfriend for chi.

✉ <u>Re: I WaS RIGHT!</u>—007UG0—aT 7:14 a.M.

I would have hooked up with Chi if I was Genesis! She'd be crazy not to. Chi is HOT. And he's smart and a top diver on the swim team. queenSheba, you are too harsh on Genesis. she would make a great girlfriend. she is a lot nicer than tasha and cj (from what i can tell in this blog). at least she's not a major bitch like them. no wonder nick and Chi liked her so much.

MOST RECENT ENTRIES   CALENDAR

VIEW FRIENDS   LINKS   PHOTOS

12/04 02:09:49

Confessions of a Boyfriend Stealer—
Blog by Genesis Bell

[15TH ENTRY]

Hate to disappoint everyone, but I said no. And I didn't plan for Chi to fall for me, I swear.

← →

I won't lie. I was totally blown away that he liked me. Let's face it, the Jan Bradys of this world do *not* attract guys like Chi. Nick was one thing, since he was such a total player, and I knew he was only chasing me because I wasn't interested (and therefore a big challenge). Chi was a different story. He was gorgeous and *deep*. When I got home from Denny's that night, I kept checking in the mirror to make sure I was still me—Genesis Bell. Chi had looked at me like I was a big deal, like maybe I was a *Marcia* Brady type. Maybe he was right, though it was hard to believe.

Despite all that, I said it would be best if we just

stayed very good friends. I'm not a total idiot. I got so burned with the Nick deal that I am never going to mess with a friend's man again. It's just wrong.

Chi was really okay with my decision, but I have a feeling he might not totally give up. I may have created a monster with all those junk-food fests, but I can handle him.

I was up early Sunday and decided I wanted to work on my documentary. Saturday had been homework day, but it had been hard for me to focus on world history and chemistry equations. Having a bizarre personal life can take its toll.

But I was now ready to totally lose myself in the world of TV production. Cher Dawson, a girl in my media class, e-mailed me an actual transcript from *Live Art*, a documentary about street performers, which was amazingly useful and interesting. She told me I should check out this Web site that lets you download real screenplays. I logged onto my PC and immediately surfed on over to Drew's Script-O-Rama (www.script-o-rama.com). I started scrolling through pages of television sitcoms and documentaries. I was getting superinspired. Maybe my theme would be something really deep, about cliques and stuff. I could interview kids who were popular and those who were on the fringes. I could follow them around and record their experiences and compare them. Maybe Fiesta Beach really would be my ticket to fame and fortune.

All I needed was some Jolt cola to keep me going.

I wandered into the kitchen and found my mother pumping iron to some spastic fitness show on TV. You usually see neither hide nor hair of her until eleven a.m. at the earliest. She always works later shifts at the salon.

It was only ten a.m., way too early for her.

I thought of asking why she was up, but then I remembered the scene with Shay the night before and decided that sometimes it's better not to know.

"Way to go for the burn, Mom," I said. She was really whaling away at those weights.

I foraged in the fridge, found a Jolt, and then grabbed a Pop-Tart from the cupboard. My mother just grunted and started pumping faster as some girl in a thong leotard pranced around on the TV screen.

I was trying to figure out if I could carry an apple on top of the Jolt and the Pop-Tart when my mother suddenly spoke.

"I don't know where Kenny is," she said in this very ominous voice. "He always goes home right after church, because he always calls me and tells me he just got home." She paused. "He usually leaves the morning service by nine-fifteen and makes it home by nine-forty-five." My mother will talk on her bedroom phone before eleven a.m., she just won't get out of bed until then.

"I thought you wanted to go to church with him." Damn, Angela was in a mood.

"Only evening services. Kenny understands that I'm not strong enough in the morning to really focus on the Lord and His message." My mother stopped and wiped her face with a paper towel. She tried to look pious but instead just looked really pissed off.

"I thought you were working later today," I said. Sometimes I forget my mother has a real job. She seems to go to the salon whenever she feels like it.

"I changed shifts with Riva," she said, frowning. "Kenny knows I rearranged things. He knows I'm here waiting to hear from him."

"He'll call you, Mom. Maybe he stopped on the way home to get Krispy Kremes or coffee or gas for the car."

She began jogging in place. "I don't know. He could have called me from his cell. He usually does that if something comes up."

I watched her try to run in place in our small kitchen. "How come you're not doing that out in the living room? It's crowded in here."

She paused to catch her breath. "Because, Genesis, he always calls our home phone when he's home. He only calls the cell when he's on his cell."

That didn't really make sense, because why not use your cell whenever? But then, honestly, older people rarely make sense to me. One of our regular phones is in the kitchen, so I guess she wanted to be close to it. I noticed my mother had her cell phone on the kitchen table too. I guess just in case Kenny broke his own rules.

"I don't like this a bit," my mother said, looking anxious. "I'm thinking of driving over to his apartment to see if he's there."

I nearly dropped everything. "What? You've always said that if you have to spy on your man, then the relationship is over."

"This time is different," she insisted. "Kenny might be sick. Kenny might need me. What if he had an accident on the slick roads?"

"All we had was a little frost last night. How bad could the roads be?"

I was really starting to think someone had slipped something into our water system. First Shay reading the Bible, and now my mother wanting to check up on her Bible-loving boyfriend.

The two of them were freaking me out.

"I think it will make you look bad, you know, desperate if you check up on him."

Bingo. The last thing my mother wants to be is desperate.

"I suppose. He is taking me out for dinner tonight, and guess where we're going?"

I didn't really want to stand there and chitchat about her trauma over Kenny while my very own TV show needed my attention.

"We're going to Le Cirque," she said proudly. "Shay recommended it. I think she's starting to come around, you know. She's not being such a pill these days."

That sounded fishy; maybe the place had been closed down for food poisoning. But I didn't have time to worry.

"Great, Mom, but I've gotta get to work."

I headed for my bedroom and my mother called out, "Don't study too hard. There's more to life than books, you know."

Earlier, I'd told Angela I was working on my documentary, but it obviously hadn't sunk in. I seriously think I'm just so much background noise to her at times.

I spent the next few hours downloading and reading more scripts, and I only took a few breaks to read e-mail and IMs.

Tasha actually texted me a couple of times. It was a little weird. I'd barely seen her and CJ since the blowout on Monday. For the rest of the week, I'd managed to get out of study hall (I said I needed to work on my documentary), and I'd avoided them during lunch by eating in the library. I think I'd spoken to the Terribles twice since Monday.

But now Tasha acted like nothing was wrong. So I acted like nothing was wrong. We both pretended to be good old Terribles. It seemed easier that way.

Tasha bugged me to go to the mall with her and CJ later, and I finally gave in. We had to face each other at some point. Maybe being surrounded by overpriced retail would help. Maybe it would all be okay.

I also IM'd Chi and assured him that I wasn't mad about Friday and that it was really cool that we were getting to be closer friends. Then Chi sent me the cutest e-card that had an Akita on it (I'd told him how much I want a dog).

Hearing from Chi made me feel great. He was a real sweetie, unlike Nick, who sent me a cyber rose and had the nerve to ask me to meet him at the Coffee Bean. Right.

Suddenly, I was feeling like I was in control. Like life was getting back on track. Feeling good made me hungry (well, I guess everything does). I realized it was lunchtime. I stumbled into the kitchen, bleary-eyed and brain-numbed. Kenny and my mother were standing there talking with their backs to the hallway. They were both dressed up, which was surprising. I thought their date was for dinner.

"Hey," I said, trying not to yawn too widely. I was glad it was only Kenny who saw me looking like a total slob—no makeup, sweats, hair in a ponytail.

I swear Kenny jumped a mile. He must have been more nervous than I thought.

"I thought you were Shay," he said.

Maybe that explained it. Shay could be scary.

"We're going out for lunch. I was so shaken up by this morning that Kenny wants to make it up to me."

"Are you guys still going to Le Cirque tonight?"

My mother looked at me as if I were insane. "Of course. I'll see you whenever, Genesis."

They headed for the door. Kenny glanced back and flushed weirdly. He wasn't my boyfriend. Not my problem.

← →

Since my mom and Kenny took her car, the Terribles came by two hours later to pick me up. Tasha was frantic to get earrings to match her iridescent shoes, and CJ wanted to talk to the person at the spa that does bikini waxes. She kept saying that this time she really wanted a Brazilian job, and I was tempted to tell her that Shay said it was worse than torture. But CJ is hard to stop once she's on a roll. CJ and Tasha were totally into themselves. Typical.

But maybe the three of us would only get back to normal if we acted normal. Maybe Nick was right and you have to lie or fake it to keep relationships healthy. Warped, I know, but I thought it could work for the Terribles.

That meant keeping my mouth shut about Chi's sudden crush on me (not that I thought Tash or CJ would believe me if I told them anyway). Of course, I wasn't breathing a word to Miss Head in the Sand about Nick's latest stunts either.

It was totally bizarre that Nick and Chi liked me at the same time. You might think I'd have felt super-conceited at this point, but for all I knew, it was a temporary situation. The two Terribles were powerful. Nick could decide he was in love with CJ after all, and Chi could go back to obsessing over Tasha. Just like that.

I slid into the backseat and noticed that CJ and Tasha were both dressed up way more than I was. Curious. CJ was driving her Jetta, and Tasha was drinking from a bottle of water and fiddling with the CD player.

CJ said, "You'll never guess what's happened!"

She'd looked in the mirror and realized she was the most obnoxious person on the planet?

"I got a job at the Fresh Squeeze Palace," she said triumphantly.

"You're kidding." CJ's family always seemed to have plenty of money, and she always got whatever she wanted without lifting a finger.

She read my mind. "It's not like I have to work, I just want to. I'll only go in eight hours a week, and it won't interfere with anything."

"And she'll get major bonus shopping points at the mall," Tasha chimed in after taking a slug of water.

Shopping points are what store employees get as extra spending cash in the mall.

"I'm sick of getting grief from my stepmom and my dad about how much I spend on clothes. This way, I can do what I want with my own money." CJ scowled into the rearview mirror. CJ often battled with her stepmom, but then she often battled with her own mom too. CJ and most women didn't mix too well.

Tasha turned around and draped herself over the front seat. "And that's not all," she said, grinning. "CJ says the manager who hired her is totally sexy."

"Dave's more than cute, he's mature. I think he's

probably nineteen. He's going to some local college or something," CJ added.

"Don't tell me. We're going by the mall and Fresh Squeeze Palace to check him out."

"Why would I bother? I already know Dave likes me. He hired me five seconds after he met me, and he took me out afterward. The assistant manager is hot too, and I think he's just Tasha's type. I'm pretty sure his name's Chad," CJ said.

She didn't even think of offering this Chad person to me?

"I might get a job there," Tasha added. She drank the rest of her water and tossed the empty bottle onto the seat.

Tasha's family had plenty of money, so she didn't need to work either. But Tasha always followed CJ's lead. If CJ was getting a job, then so was Tasha.

"After the interview, Dave took me to this really awesome microbrewery," CJ gushed. "He told me he'd never met anyone like me before." Of course CJ got into a microbrewery even if she was underage. Of course.

"What about Nick? Aren't you guys still together?"

CJ glanced in the mirror again and gave me a dirty look. "What about him? And why do *you* care?"

"I don't. It's not my problem, is it?"

She tossed her head. "I'm not worried about Nick."

Hah! She should be. Not that I took Nick's chasing me as a serious sign of love.

She and I glared at each other some more by means of the rearview mirror.

Tasha broke the tension by saying, "Listen, before you say anything, I know that Chi is totally sweet, but we're not serious or anything. He knows I talk to other guys."

Tasha was so clueless about Chi. It was pathetic. She didn't even see him as a person who might want to "talk" to other girls or might even like other girls (ahem).

"In other words, Genesis, you've got nothing to worry about. Tash and I know how to take care of our men," CJ said in a very snippy voice.

I had to restrain myself from strangling her. We all were quiet for a second, and then I had a sudden revelation.

"I don't suppose you guys asked about a job for me at Fresh Squeeze," I said. Not that I had my own transportation, but we could have worked something out.

CJ tossed her head. "I'd think mixing smoothies would be beneath a big film producer."

Tasha piped up. "Sorry, Gen, but they're only going to hire one more person." Of course that person had to be Tasha, Miss Moneybags, not me.

"Nice how it works out for you two," I said. Now I wanted to smack them both.

"Don't be a baby about it," CJ said. "We can't force them to hire you."

She really was on my last nerve. Maybe I'd let her get that Brazilian bikini wax after all.

As for the three of us getting back to the way we used to be, that wasn't happening today. I wondered if it would ever happen. Or if I even wanted it to.

MESSAGE BOARD

✉ WE ALL JUMPED TO CONCLUSIONS—007ugo—AT 8:39 P.M.

Genesis was so cool about Chi! I mean, she turned him down—and he is SO fine. I would have fallen right into his arms! ;-) queenSheba, you were way too harsh on her. You should say you are sorry. I really wonder why genesis didn't tell CJ and Tasha to go to hell after they bragged about their new boyfriends. Gross. I'd have told them goodbye forever.

✉ RE: WE ALL JUMPED TO CONCLUSIONS—JUICYFRUIT45—AT 8:46 P.M.

You are so right, 007ugo. We just figured Genesis would go crazy over Chi. we were wrong. Why can't I meet a guy like Chi? the guys in my school are so immature. anyway, I hope someday genesis and chi do get together.

✉ RE: WE ALL JUMPED TO CONCLUSIONS—QUEENSHEBA—AT 9:18 P.M.

i admit i was too harsh on genesis. but once a girl hurts

her reputation, it's hard for her to get it back. i was glad she didn't dump her friends. no matter what.

✉ Re: we all jumped to conclusions—
JUICYFRUIT45—at 10:11 p.m.
If I had friends turning on me and guys chasing me, I could not deal with making a television show. I wonder if she just wanted to bag fiesta beach. I probably would have.

MOST RECENT ENTRIES CALENDAR

VIEW FRIENDS LINKS PHOTOS

13/04 03:25:18

CONFESSIONS OF A BOYFRIEND STEALER—
BLOG BY GENESIS BELL

[16TH ENTRY]

No way was I going to give up my documentary. This was going to be my big career move and my ticket out of Jamaica Plains someday! Even if I ended up friendless and loveless, I'd have fame and fortune to look forward to.

← →

Fiesta Beach was coming up too fast, and I was getting nervous. It seemed like the whole world was psyched about it. Fortis told me that kids from other schools wanted to come to the party after hearing about my show. God.

Wednesday in media lab, Cher Dawson sat down next to me. Fiesta Beach was in ten days, and I was trying not to gnaw my fingernails to death.

Cher is kind of Goth-looking but cool. She and I

were always friendly but only to a point. Cher made it clear she despised Tash and CJ.

"Hey, Gen," she said, playing with the piercing in her nose. I winced because it looked like she was about to take out a nostril. "I just wanted to tell you that if you want to borrow my black velvet cape, feel free. You'd really stand out, and that's what producers want, right?"

I choked out, "Uh, yeah, that's true, but it might kind of get in the way. I'm not sure I'm coordinated enough to handle a cape and a camera."

"That's cool. I think this party is gonna rock. I can't wait to see your film." She grinned broadly, exposing a diamond-inlaid tooth.

"Thanks." I was relieved she wasn't hurt that I turned down her cape.

Her grin turned into a grimace. "But you'd better not let those witches dominate the show, Genesis, or everyone will be seriously pissed." She got up and shot me a dark, Goth look. "I mean it."

I shrugged. If only Cher knew how shaky the Terrible alliance really was.

I was seeing CJ and Tasha all the time, unfortunately. They were seriously getting on my nerves, especially CJ. She couldn't stop talking about stupid Dave. She claimed he was chasing her day and night. I wished I could say it was all a big ego trip on her part, but it probably wasn't. Guys were always chasing CJ. She was so obnoxious that I had to do something (especially since the topic of Nick was off limits). So I ragged on her about chickening out on the Brazilian bikini wax. She could only turn red and not say a word because she knew she'd wussed out. Too bad. If anyone deserved a Brazilian bikini wax it was CJ.

By Friday she was really irritating me to death. She was taking bitchiness to a whole new level. I'd never been CJ's target before, so I hadn't minded so much when she was in attack mode. But now, since the whole Nick mess, I was getting the full brunt of her nasty attitude. And I didn't like it at all.

We were eating lunch at this veggie place down the street from our school. I should say Tasha and I were eating while CJ was playing with her wrap.

"Dave is so cool," she was saying. "So much more grown-up than most guys we know. He bought me this really sexy toe ring. It has a real emerald in it." She smirked at Tasha and me.

Okay, we were both impressed because she had scored real jewelry after knowing the guy less than a week.

"I think I might even be falling for him," CJ said. "Like in love."

I think she was showing off, but I restrained myself from dumping my Coke on her.

"Dave is just so incredible," she gushed. "I'm not kidding. He's so awesome. I may have to break up with Nick."

Neither Tasha nor CJ had actually started working at the Fresh Squeeze Palace, but it didn't matter. They already had these new guys wrapped around their little fingers.

"So why don't you, then?" I sounded really bitchy, and even Tasha stared at me.

"Because it's too soon to know about Dave, if you don't mind." CJ made her voice just as bitchy as mine.

I think Tasha figured out things were getting nasty between CJ and me and decided it was time to jump in and break up the catfight.

"Guess what. Chad called me last night," she said. She grinned. "Right after he brought me home from employee training. He wants to take me somewhere great. I told him Fiesta Beach is the best party of the year."

I couldn't believe Tasha. "What about Chi? Aren't you going with him?" She so didn't deserve Chi. No wonder he wanted to hang out with me—after all that abuse.

"Well, yeah, I know. I told Chad I might have to go with my boyfriend, and he totally understood." She paused to stuff herself. "He mentioned his prom at Overton High—which is, by the way, known to be cool and full of gorgeous guys. Anyway, Chad said he'd get a limo and a private suite at the Hilton and everything."

Can you see how the world sucks? Tasha and CJ are spoiled rotten and treat guys like crap, yet they get emerald toe rings and luxury prom packages.

Watching CJ maul her veggie wrap was making me sick, so maybe that's why I said what I said. "Did you know emeralds are only valuable if they're a certain color and grade?"

(I was making this up. I really don't know jack about emeralds.)

CJ glared at me. "What's your point, Genesis? You haven't even seen my new toe ring."

I shrugged. "I was just saying. It's no big deal." Like I wanted to see the crummy jewelry she was getting from some loser at the FSP!

"I took it to a jewelry store to make it smaller, and they said it was really expensive."

Tasha stopped eating. "How come he bought such a big toe ring for you?"

"He didn't," CJ snapped. "I happen to have extra tiny feet."

She was lying or on drugs. CJ might be a size two, but she has feet like the abominable snowman. I think they're thirteens or something.

CJ isn't happy unless she's making everyone else jealous.

Tasha was adding extra dressing to her salad, and CJ was wincing (Angela says dressing is the enemy since it's full of hidden calories). "I can't stop thinking about Chad. He's so hot that's he's scorching," Tasha panted. She giggled and fanned herself.

"So bring him to the party," CJ said. "Have both Chad and Chi come by themselves at different times; tell them you'll meet them there. Andy's house is huge, and it'll be so packed that you'll be able to keep both guys busy—and apart." She snickered. "The only thing is you'll have to stay sober enough to juggle them. Oh, and make sure one goes home earlier—by himself."

I couldn't believe her. No wonder all the girls at Jamaica Plains High hated her guts.

"I guess, but I'm not ready to totally lose Chi, and if he sees me and Chad together on Genesis's documentary, he'll end it."

CJ scowled at me. "So tell Ms. Producer to keep her stupid camera away."

"I can't chance it. Gen could catch me and Chad in some background shot by accident. It's one thing for Chi to hear about me and another guy, but seeing it with his own eyes . . ." Tasha shook her head.

"I really don't see how Ms. Producer can get away with filming us without getting some kind of release forms, anyway," CJ said.

She was pushing it. "Fortis is posting signs everywhere to let people know." I gripped my Coke hard. "Everyone is really into it, anyway."

Man, did I have self-control. I made myself take a drink. "Anyway, it's up to Tasha to deal with this."

"I do love Chi, you know, but I'm too young to be tied down." That's what older people always say. At least Tasha looked a little guilty for repeating such crap. "I guess I'll just go with Chi to Fiesta Beach. Chad and everything will have to wait till afterwards." She sighed. "Chad said he'd buy my prom dress, did I tell you? He said we could go to Saks."

They were making me sick. I wished I had earplugs. Anything to block them out.

CJ reached over to high-five Tasha. "Way to go, girl. Just make sure he pays full retail, and accept no markdowns or sales." She and Tasha giggled.

"We can drive together if you want, Tash. That way, Nick doesn't have to obsess over DUIs, since Chi likes being Mr. Designated," CJ said.

Tasha slurped her smoothie. "Chi likes to party, but he doesn't overdo it." She paused for another slurp. "Hey, make sure Nick brings that new hangover stuff, Finito. I hear it really works if you take it an hour or two after you've had some drinks."

"I'll remind him," CJ said. She poked at her scrawny stomach and frowned at imaginary fat. "Even though, I don't know. I don't mind throwing up after partying. It really cleanses your system and makes you lose a few pounds."

I loved hearing about the benefits of hurling after I'd just eaten a drippy veggie wrap. The conversation was getting to me, and I was glad when lunch was finally over.

I'd had enough of the Terribles for one day (maybe forever!). While CJ drove us back to school, she and Tasha talked nonstop about how they were starting work at the Fresh Squeeze Palace the next day and how Dave and Chad were taking them out afterward. Chad and Dave. Talk about stupid names. I've never trusted anyone named Dave, and I thought Chad was just a name for guys on soap operas.

I was late for chemistry class, and it was CJ's fault for taking so long to dissect her lunch. I tried to slink unnoticed into the room, but everyone stared at me like they'd never seen someone walk in tardy before. Mr. Elfman glared at me but didn't say a word. Nick grinned at me from the back of the class and waved.

I ignored him and slid into my seat. Someone tapped me on the shoulder. I turned, and Bill Fielder, a basketball jock who usually sleeps through class, handed me a note. I opened it.

It said:

I have a yen
for my sexy Gen.
Just give me a chance,
babe, I'll even dance.
Love, Nick

Omigod. How corny could you get? Nick probably thought I'd melt. Right. Of course, if I showed CJ the note, she'd insist I'd written it myself.

I turned around, and Nick winked at me. God, he had a nerve. I was so tempted to throw something at him, but Elfman was shooting me the evil eye.

Later, Chi IM'd me during class and asked if I wanted to meet him at Dog Eat Dog Records (it's a really hip alternative music store) that night. I said yeah because I knew we'd have an awesome time, and besides, anything was better than hanging out at home. My mother was supertense about Kenny, and my sister wasn't speaking to anyone. Fun.

Chi wanted me to listen to a new techno group called KYO. He'd invited Tasha (still his official girlfriend) first, but she was busy and even suggested that he ask me to go. She still sees me as a Jan Brady.

Shay was working, and my mom was going out with Kenny and said I could use her Mustang.

Dog Eat Dog Records tends to attract really alternative people, but I didn't care. Chi and I would have a great time in a purely alternative way.

MESSAGE BOARD

✉ I LOVE DOG EAT DOG AND KYO!—007ugo—AT 1:34 A.M.

Genesis has such good taste in music. So does Chi. (too bad Chi wasn't the one to write the love poem instead of Nick!) I think Genesis and Chi should be a real couple someday.

✉ RE: I LOVE DOG EAT DOG AND KYO!—JUICYFRUIT45—AT 1:59 A.M.

I've never been to Dog Eat Dog, but I love KYO. I think Genesis should end up with Chi someday too. I wonder if she was even tempted to kiss him? I would have been! Maybe she did and isn't telling anyone.

MOST RECENT ENTRIES   CALENDAR
VIEW FRIENDS   LINKS   PHOTOS

14/04 05:03:44

CONFESSIONS OF A BOYFRIEND STEALER—
BLOG BY GENESIS BELL

[17TH ENTRY]

I swear I didn't lock lips with Chi (even though he's got an incredibly sexy mouth). Remember, I promised to tell the whole truth, no matter how revolting (remember Nick and Sherryn). I had to keep my mind on business; the weekend was over.

← →

Usually Mondays are crap days for the obvious reasons: No sleeping in. No stuffing your face whenever you want. No goofing off and spending the day in your pajamas. But this Monday was different. This entire week was different. Fiesta Beach, the social event of the year, was happening on Saturday. No one talked about anything else. I mean nothing else. I should have been super-freaked-out, considering, but I was distracted.

I was still thinking about what an amazing time

Chi and I had that Friday night. We had listened to tons of emo and techno music. We both loved edgy stuff like Enigma, Zara, and Dis. Chi and I really got along. It was great having someone around who understood me. I know he wanted more, but he respected how I felt, so he didn't pull a Nick. He didn't try to kiss me or anything. (We didn't talk about Nick either. That subject was closed!)

We were going to stay platonic, even if it killed me. Monday morning in media lab I was reminding myself that I'd better get serious about my role as TV producer of the social event of the year when Cher tapped me on the shoulder. "I am so ready for Saturday. Look."

She flipped up her shirt. She'd added a second piercing to her belly button. One was bad enough, but two was too gross for words. But she was being nice to me, so I tried to control my gag reflex as I admired her reddened, puffy, bruised white stomach. I wish I weren't so squeamish. Body mutilation is totally in, and I can't even bear to get my ears pierced.

I said something like "Oh, that's nice," and she wandered back to her seat.

The week flew by way too quickly. I felt like I needed more time, but I realized that I'd actually figured out most of the special features of my Sony. Okay, I couldn't do them all, but I didn't really need echoing sound effects or filtered lighting. I could make things fuzzy and herky-jerky and even figured out how to superimpose images. It was going to be so cool.

I had been wracking my brain over my theme, and I decided to really make the party dynamics the story. In other words, the theme would be apparent after the party was over. I decided I'd just wander around the Fortis house as the spirit moved me, but I'd be sure to get shots of people coming in, people on the floor, and people hanging around the food and drinks.

My nerves had kicked in again. I told myself my show would turn out awesome, but my stomach didn't believe that. Genesis Bell, the famous turbo-eater, was unable to chow down per usual.

By the time Friday came around, I was so jumpy and hyped that I could barely sit still. Drinking gallons of Coke and Jolt probably didn't help.

Of course, CJ was so supportive. Not! At lunch, she said, "Jesus, Genesis, it's not like you're Steven Spielberg trying for an Oscar. Why don't you just get a grip? You've been a pain in the ass all week. And, that's your third Coke—what are you, a caffeine freak suddenly?"

I deliberately slurped hard on my straw, making a loud, obnoxious noise. But I didn't answer. CJ was still superpissed about my and Nick's hooking up over break (even though she still wasn't admitting that it had happened), and I was still superpissed about her treating me like a loser.

Plus, CJ was a huge hypocrite since she was ready to dump Nick's ass and hook up with her Fresh Squeeze doofus.

Tasha said, "I'm trying to decide if I should wear my black thong bikini or my white one. I don't know."

"It all depends on how tan you're going to be. Are you going to that spray-on place again this week?" CJ was studying Tasha as if she were about to perform brain surgery on her.

Tasha held out her golden brown arms. "I may squeeze in one more visit. Black is sexier, but white looks so good with a tan."

I almost told her that she'd look hot in either bikini but bit my tongue. I was not going there. Maybe months before—okay, weeks before—I would have been flattering and reassuring Tasha and CJ like crazy.

CJ pulled a bottle of shark fin pills (how appropriate) from her purse. CJ had read somewhere that they make you thin, and she believed this because she said she'd never seen a fat shark. "I'm bringing my gold suit and my pink one. The gold is too expensive to spill anything on it, so I can change after a while," CJ said. "Oh, I finally realized that Nick and I are *over*. We just haven't talked about it. I figure after the party, we'll end it." She paused to swallow a pill. "But it all works out, 'cause Dave's way too mature for high school parties anyway."

But not too mature for high school girls, I almost said.

I stared at Tasha and CJ. How could they have turned into such shallow bitches? I know. They were always like that. But we'd been the *three* Terribles.

Maybe I was a Terrible no longer, or I never was one, or I was having a Terrible meltdown.

Message Board

✉ I WONDER—JUICYFRUIT45—aT 11:23 P.M.
if CJ and Tasha ever cared at all about Nick and Chi. All they talked about were these new boyfriends.

✉ Re: I WONDER—007ugo—aT 12:02 a.M.
No way. They just wanted to own them. I used to see CJ hanging all over Nick. Tasha did the same with Chi. It was just for show, because they'd flirt like crazy when those guys weren't around. Totally two-faced and slutty.

✉ Re: I WONDER—QueenSHeba—aT 12:47 a.M.
my stupid computer was on the blink again! grrrrr >:-< had to catch up on everything. glad i didn't miss anything big! like hearing that genesis really hadn't kissed chi after all. i know cj and tasha aren't perfect, but they were genesis's friends for a long time. that counts for something in my book. if i were her, i'd have been worried that i was losing the terribles.

15/04 01:15:21

CONFESSIONS OF A BOYFRIEND STEALER— BLOG BY GENESIS BELL

[18TH ENTRY]

I was not going to let the Terribles ruin everything for me, so I had to put them on a back burner. Sometimes you gotta prioritize. Worrying about CJ and Tasha and how they treated boyfriends and nonboyfriends was just not on the list!

← →

It was the Big Day: *Fiesta Beach Day.* In twelve hours, at approximately nine p.m., the biggest social event of the year would be launched, and so would my "groundbreaking" (I'm quoting Mr. Nichols) documentary and maybe my TV production career. I would arrive early, at eight o'clock. I wanted to practice using the camcorder in that enormous house and get a read on the lighting. I also wanted to make sure I could handle it without tripping or running into furniture. Oh God!

The night before, Angela and Shay had taken a break from their Kenny drama long enough to advise me on my wardrobe. The consensus was that I should wear a sarong and a bikini top instead of the standard two-piece bikini. Shay pointed out that not only would the sarong make me look taller, but I also wouldn't have to worry about wedgies while I was running around filming everything. Angela pointed out that wearing something different from the rest of the partiers would make me look more professional.

I decided to take their advice; as ex–beauty queens, they really do know a few tricks of the entertainment trade. I got out of bed and reached for my stuffed Akita to hug, and then grabbed my ancient stuffed spaniel for additional comfort. I needed all the reassurance I could get. For a second, I thought of calling Tasha or CJ . . . but only for a second.

That night was going to be huge.

I closed my eyes and tried to mentally rehearse how to use the special camcorder features. Maybe I'd reread the manual once more. Someone was talking and moving around in the living room, which ruined my concentration. I strained to listen. Angela. That made two weekends in a row she was up early. Very weird. I tiptoed out into the hall.

Shay was nowhere to be seen and her bed was still made, so I guessed she'd spent the night at a bar friend's house or at EJ's or Justin's. I peeked out the window and saw her Jeep parked near the street. She'd grudgingly agreed to let me use it that night and gotten one of her love slaves to chauffeur her around. Now I could hear my mother on the phone moaning to one of her girlfriends (she actually has a few of them) about Kenny.

I was starting to believe she really did have a thing for the God dude in plaid. I mean, Kenny seems pretty sweet, but that usually doesn't matter with my mother.

I snuck into the bathroom because I didn't want Angela to know I was up yet and slathered on some facial mask of Shay's.

I waited fifteen minutes and washed the mask off. I had to admire how it made my complexion brighter and smoother. Even my hair looked great somehow. I was definitely camera ready. Now, if only Angela would give me the space and quiet that I needed to psyche myself up.

I was going to play with my hair and see if a little mousse would give it more body when my mother banged on the bathroom door.

"Genesis, I'm leaving. I can't stay around here anymore. I've had it."

Her voice was trembling, and her fake Southern accent was fading. This sounded dangerously serious. I really didn't want to open the door, but I knew I'd better. If I didn't, she'd keep right on talking through the door, and I wouldn't get any privacy anyway.

"I refuse to be a helpless victim another second," my mother was saying as I opened the door. She was wearing her big chandelier earrings. They practically hang down to her shoulders and they're all glittery and covered with little diamonds. She only wears them for special occasions. I wouldn't be caught dead in them, even though they're expensive. They are so Home Shopping Network meets country-western singer.

I noticed she was wearing her power suit too. It's bright pink and supershort. Usually you won't catch Angela dead in anything remotely resembling business attire.

Something cold crept up my spine. Thoughts of Fiesta Beach faded for the moment. The last time I saw Angela in a suit was when she went after Shay's father for some money he owed her. She was ready to drag him to Judge Judy (www.judgejudy.com) and make his life hell until he finally coughed up the dough. He paid her, all right.

"Sometimes a woman has to do what a woman has to do," she continued now, as if she were giving a speech.

I started to ask her what was up, but then she said, "Kenny was very withdrawn last night, and he barely kissed me goodnight. Then he brought me home early. And now"—she paused for a breath—"and now he's stood me up. We're supposed to have breakfast at the Hilton. They have that buffet with a harp player, and all the fixin's."

Her Southern accent was creeping back in, and her face was getting really flushed.

"No one stands me up, Genesis," she hissed.

Somehow, I couldn't picture Kenny messing around

or cheating on her. He was a Jesus guy. There had to be some explanation.

I opened my mouth, then closed it. I had my own life to stress about.

"Don't try to stop me, Genesis. That man's going to tell me what's going on, or my name's not Angela Bell." She was breathing hard now.

Poor Kenny.

She smiled a scary smile before charging off. Seconds later, I heard her slam out of the house. If I were braver, I might have tried to convince her not to hunt down Kenny, because I thought she was making a huge mistake. But no one stops Angela Bell when she's raring to go. I heard the Mustang burn rubber and peel out.

Yes, Angela forgot about my show and the party that night, but I didn't really care. I was relieved that she was out of the house. I knew whatever was going down with her and Kenny would be worked out one way or another. Either Kenny would be kicked to the curb, or Angela would come home with new jewelry. I was betting on the latter.

I spent the rest of the morning practicing with my camcorder and trying different hairstyles. Should I go wild and wavy à la MTV or sleek and ponytailed à la CNN? I decided to go CNN. I was the producer, after all.

No sign of Angela, which probably meant she and Kenny were making up in some fancy restaurant.

After lunch, I didn't get much chance to focus on anything because I was busy talking on the phone and answering e-mail. First, Chi e-mailed me a really nice note and an e-card of an open bottle of champagne that spouted out bubbles spelling the words GOOD LUCK! He said that he knew my show was going to be huge.

Then I got an e-mail from Nick, who offered to come over and give me a back rub—to relax me. What an egomaniac.

My master plan was to add my free-floating commentary to the footage of the party. I so didn't want to be a dork commentator-host.

At seven, I was about to leave for Fortis's house when Tasha called.

"CJ wanted me to remind you about the lighting," she said breathlessly. "She doesn't want to look fat on TV."

I said, "Tell CJ not to worry. I've got everything under control. Even her imaginary fat." I wanted to get off the phone fast.

"I'm so excited," Tasha said. "I went for one more spray-on tan session, and I look really dark."

"I'm so pale I look like I'm from *The Addams Family*," I said, squeezing out a lame laugh.

I rushed Tasha off the phone, hung up, grabbed my stuff, and raced out to Shay's Jeep. I was wearing a long coat over the sarong and bikini top, and my high-tops. I had my mike, my notes, my emergency makeup kit, hair spray, and my emergency M&M's in a duffel bag.

As I drove, I tried some deep breathing exercises that I'd read were good for reducing stress. I am cool and calm. I am cool and calm. If I said it enough times, maybe I'd believe it.

MESSAGE BOARD

✉ FAMILIES—007UGO—AT 10:06 P.M.
I wonder if Gen's family is for real? I know she said she would tell the truth, but you have to wonder. Compared to the Bells, my mom and stepdad are totally normal. They would have asked me a zillion questions about the party! They probably would have given me a superlong lecture and crap.

✉ RE: FAMILIES—JUICYFRUIT45—AT 10:23 P.M.
I know! my mom would never even let me go to fiesta beach. she'd worry about drinking and everyone being in bathing suits.

✉ RE: FAMILIES—QUEENSHEBA—AT 11:32 P.M.
I can't believe genesis's mom didn't give her a curfew or anything. My parents would have!

MOST RECENT ENTRIES   CALENDAR
VIEW FRIENDS   LINKS   PHOTOS

17/04 11:03:49

CONFESSIONS OF A BOYFRIEND STEALER—
BLOG BY GENESIS BELL

[19TH ENTRY]

This sounds scary, but I'm used to my family. It would have been way weird if Angela had started interrogating me about Fiesta Beach (or my documentary). I was just glad I could put their Kenny drama out of my head, because I was so ready for my big night. I just wanted it to start.

← →

At first, everyone at the party acted like I was taping a *Girls Gone Wild.* Julie Santos and Monica Fargo, two juniors on the varsity cheer squad, flipped up their bikini tops for my camera (Julie obviously liked tanning in the buff—no strap marks—and Monica had a nipple ring, ugh). Not that I was checking them out, but it's hard to avoid breasts when they're right in your face. Julie and Monica weren't even drunk; they were just acting like spazzes because of the camera. Then they started booty dancing. By now, I was feeling the party mood. I was a lot more relaxed. Right at nine, Fiesta Beach had started popping, which is typical. Most parties take forever to get off the ground, but people come to Fiesta Beach primed for action. As soon as I started filming, I was totally fine, and the nervousness went away.

Julie and Monica continued to dance and pose for the camera, topless. I said into the mike, "Is this a new trend in cheerleading? I'm sure the football team would approve."

At least in a *Girls Gone Wild* video, Julie and Monica would have gotten free T-shirts. I'd just end up editing them and their bared boobs right out of the show. I didn't want cheesy, show-offy stuff—you know, like the crap you see on home movies and wedding videos. I wanted the real nitty-gritty Fiesta Beach moments, not idiots acting idiotic for the camera. But at first that's all I was getting. Andy Fortis kept jumping in front of the camera in his baggy swim trunks and baseball cap, trying some lame rap and dance routine à la Eminem (Slim Shady should sue). Then Mike Feller started yelling and belly flopping onto the sand-covered floor. He looked up at me like I should be impressed. Not. Moron city.

I was so glad I wore my sarong skirt, because I could work the room without worrying about sucking in my stomach or freaking out over bikini-bottom wedgies.

The Fortis mansion was totally packed. There had

to be a couple of hundred people streaming through the ten rooms on the first floor. So far, I hadn't spotted Tash, CJ, Nick, or Chi. I know Tasha and CJ love dramatic entrances, which is why they're always late. I checked the front door a few times but didn't see the Terribles or their men. The party was getting bigger and wilder. You couldn't move without touching someone's nearly naked body. Sometimes that was a good thing; other times, not.

Suddenly, the reggae music got really loud and a couple of Andy's friends brought out more bowls of punch, which everyone said were spiked to the max. Some of the senior guys were setting up the limbo stick and yelling for people to line up. Everyone started drifting toward them and towards the booze. I heard strains of "Limbo Rock" start up too. They'd be alternating between it and "Limbo Louie," which meant we'd be hearing both songs a million times.

About forty-five minutes had gone by, and the novelty of being filmed for a documentary was wearing off a little. Thank God! Two seniors, Malinda Davies and Jenecia Stern, walked right near me. They were deep in conversation, and luckily, they were loud.

"You tell the Boomer that if he wants me, then he'll have to apologize for acting like a jerk last night. He treated me like I was invisible when his friends stopped by, and I don't appreciate it." Malinda glanced at me and went right on talking. She was too hopped up over her relationship woes to care about me and my camera. "Besides, whenever I tell him that I love him, he just says 'Thanks, man.' He never tells me he loves me."

Malinda should know never to expect romance from a guy who calls himself the Boomer.

"But he's so sorry, Mal," Jenecia said. "At least let me tell him you'll talk to him—"

I said into the mike, "Everyone is so into love here. Too bad we spend all our time chasing it or fighting over it . . . instead of getting it. . . ." I was getting good at this commentary.

Things were finally starting to roll. One of the drama club guys had brought a karaoke machine and used it to practice his monologue from Shakespeare (something about death and love and tortured souls— typical Shakespeare, from what I've seen). He stood up on the Fortises' expensive-looking coffee table and performed for about a minute. He got some applause but mostly boos. He was pretty good, but you gotta consider the audience. Someone always brings karaoke, even though you'd think they'd learn.

I added my own thoughts. "Some kids take themselves really seriously, as you can see, but artsy speeches at Fiesta Beach? C'mon. Don't forget—in high school, if you bleed, they'll eat you alive." Nice imagery, huh?

Two guys almost got into a fistfight over doing the limbo. One swore the other touched the ground with his pinky, and the other swore he didn't. One of the beefier senior guys had to break it up. Limbo is taken really seriously at Fiesta Beach.

Some guy and two girls were dirty dancing together. They looked like they were auditioning for a porn movie. The girls started kissing each other to the wild cheers of some of the guys watching. Typical Fiesta Beach; fake lesbian action is another tradition.

Cher came by to ask how I was doing. I knew she was still disappointed that I hadn't worn her cape. As a consolation, I let her flash her double-pierced belly button.

Through it all, I made more editorial comments and invited some of my fellow partiers to talk with me on camera. So many people are hams. I was also really glad that I'd practiced using the special features of my camcorder, especially the panoramic and the fish-eye shots. I got some great fade-outs and shadowy sequences too.

So far, I had captured two major girl arguments, a breakup-and-makeup (both within fifteen minutes), and another performance on the karaoke machine.

It was all going great—the whole night was perfect. So far.

MESSAGE BOARD

✉ FIESTA BEACH—007U9O—AT 10:06 P.M.
It sounds so amazing. I'm sorry I missed all the Fiesta Beaches. I'm graduating, so maybe I can go to the next one when I come home from college. I hope so. I can't wait to see Genesis's film!

✉ Re: Fiesta Beach—JUICYFRUIT45—at 10:23 p.m.

I know you said you didn't like big parties, 007ugo. Maybe it's more fun to hear about it, or to watch it on TV ☺. Genesis must have had such an awesome time. I wish I could have been her for that one night. It would have been so cool to make a movie and have everyone admire what you were doing.

✉ Re: Fiesta Beach—QUEENSHEBA—at 11:01 p.m.

i agree. i would love to have been in her shoes too. i am definitely going to fiesta beach next year. i think it's better than prom! genesis was so lucky.

18/04 07:34:06

CONFESSIONS OF A BOYFRIEND STEALER— BLOG BY GENESIS BELL

[20TH ENTRY]

It's not like I was the star of Fiesta Beach or anything. People just loved being on camera, and I happened to be the one behind the lens. I admit it felt kind of cool being in a position of power like that, but it was also weird not being with CJ and Tasha.

It must have been eleven or so, and I was dying of thirst. I still hadn't seen Chi or Nick or the Terribles. I snagged a glass of punch (only my second) and tried not to gulp it. I was limiting myself because a professional can't allow herself to get drunk on the job. Not that I'm a big drinker anyway. If I hadn't been working, I might have three or four drinks at the most. Anyway, the punch was so spiked that it practically made my tongue bleed.

I took a deep breath. I was feeling really good. I was

handling the camera well, and I couldn't wait to see how it all looked after—

Cold hands grabbed my waist. I shrieked and dropped my punch on the floor, splattering my sarong. I spun around.

It was Nick, the dog, in baggy swim trunks and a wife-beater. He looked good, I admit. Not that I cared.

"What the hell are you doing?" I shouted.

Nick grinned at me. "What do you think I'm doing? Saying hello to my goil . . ."

Oh no, not *The Sopranos* again. Plus, that line was for CJ; I don't like secondhand come-ons. And he was obviously wasted.

"Where is everyone?" I meant where was CJ, and why didn't she have a leash on her drunk-ass boyfriend? I craned my neck but didn't see her or Tasha or Chi.

Nick threw his arm around my neck and nearly knocked me down. "Don't know. But I think they went that-a-way." He waved in some vague direction. "My man Chi was looking for food, and CJ and Tasha were looking for the bathroom to do their makeup." He laughed like he thought he'd said something funny. Typical drunk.

I searched once more for CJ and Tash, but I knew they could be ages. Beauty maintenance was serious work for those two.

"When did you guys get here?" I couldn't shift his arm, so I tried to look cool, though we were in this really klutzy embrace. I really wasn't into babysitting

CJ's boyfriend anymore; I wished she'd show up and take him off my hands. Not that she'd ever *want* to believe that Nick was flirting with me. She'd probably just tell me I was delusional again. She'd probably insist that Nick was just being friendly or some such crap. It would absolutely kill her ego to admit the truth.

" 'Bout twenty minutes ago. Chi drove us all here. . . . We stopped at the Blue Circle first."

So that was why he was already plastered.

"Nick, I'm here to work, okay? So why don't you go wait somewhere for CJ?"

He pouted. "Don't be mean, Gen. I'm just happy to see you . . . and besides, CJ and everyone will be looking for me real soon, 'cause I got this." He showed me the bottle of Finito, the hangover preventive, tucked in his shorts pocket.

"I just wanted a special moment alone with you." Then he grinned and gave me a big bear hug. We were so off balance we almost fell.

Oh God. I'd forgotten to turn off the camera. Of course, the visuals would be wildly out of focus, but the audio would be okay. I struggled to hit the Stop button, but the next thing I knew Nick was dragging me across the room. "Let's go limbo, baby. *How low can you go!*" He shouted right in my ear and nearly deafened me. Oh yeah, this was real special.

A couple of times I tried to pull my arm free, but Nick only held on tighter. I sighed and gave up. This couldn't last much longer. Drunks have short attention spans. I'd lose him in a minute.

We bumbled through the crowd. "I'm going to kill you," I said through gritted teeth.

"C'mon, be my goil, Gen. Do one limbo with me, okay? Look, we're already here."

I was so not his "goil"! But Nick had pulled me to the end of the limbo line. Oh yeah, and someone was cranking up "Limbo Louie." One trip under the stupid pole and I was out of there. I wasn't spending a second longer with Nick Pilates than I had to. Besides, I was a total spaz when it came to limboing.

I could still turn the camcorder off . . . but I had sworn that this show would be brutally honest. Damn, sometimes it sucks being ethical. I set the camcorder on a nearby chair. The footage would be useless, nothing but blurred legs and out-of-focus navels, but the audio would capture everything.

I watched a bunch of people fall on their butts trying to snake their way under the limbo stick. Each time someone crash-landed, the crowd watching would hoot and boo. Only Darcy Fields and Kimmy Soo, who were both on the gymnastics team, succeeded. They not only made it look easy, but they also looked perfect in their bikinis. They smiled smugly when they got huge applause. Show-offs.

In a second, it would be Nick's turn. I folded my arms and tapped my foot. I really didn't need this. I had to take a few more shots of people dancing—

Suddenly, I was being pulled forward by the wrist. The two guys holding the bar grinned. I tried to dig my heels in, but Nick was too strong. What the hell was he doing?

He and I were right in front of the limbo stick (which was only about waist high). And we were really close to a speaker, so I could hear some of the annoying lyrics.

"Limbo up and limbo down . . ."

"Go for it, Pilates," yelled one of the idiots holding the bar.

"Limbo Louie never frown . . ."

"It's double limbo time! Two for the price of one!" Nick shouted back. "Let's get down, Gen! Let's show 'em how good we are, babe!" He winked at me and pulled me closer.

Omigod. That sounded suggestive. We'd only kissed, not done the nasty. I spotted Cher and a few other girls I knew gawking at me like I was a total sleaze.

"Shake your tush and don't fall down . . ."

I couldn't pull free. Everyone was laughing and clapping so loud I could barely hear lyrics anymore. Double limbo was a new trick, so it had to be exciting. Not. If I screamed or made a fuss, I'd look like an idiotic wimp. Crap.

The next thing I knew Nick and I were trying to slide together under the stupid bar. I was bending backward and not falling . . . I was keeping my balance. I was doing it. . . . Then Nick's feet shot out from under him when he stepped on a bunch of ice. Some jerk had spilled his drink right under the limbo stick, turning the sand into slippery mud. Nick fell, taking the bar and me with him.

Nick landed on his back, and somehow I flipped over and crashed facedown—right on top of him. Ice cubes were all around us. I tried to get up, but the breath was knocked out of me. And Nick was holding on for dear life. Maybe he thought he was drowning or something. The surprisingly heavy limbo stick was digging into my back. Reluctantly, I snuck a peek and noticed that everyone was staring down at us.

I heard *"Shake your tush . . ."* and then silence. Someone turned the music off.

It was starting to feel like I'd be stuck on top of Nick forever. People were laughing and making jokes. (I was so glad I was wearing a sarong skirt. I couldn't imagine the cheek exposure otherwise.)

Then some genius yelled, "Hey, you two, get a room!"

Nick looked up at me and said, "Gen, you are so sexy." Then he hiccupped.

Someone let out a gasp, followed by a shriek.

A familiar voice suddenly bellowed out, "You ho! Get your fat ass off my boyfriend!"

Another familiar voice followed. "Genesis! How could you!"

Then, omigod, it was Chi. "Genesis! Is that you?"

The first was CJ, Miss Anorexica, Miss Snot, and Miss Hypocrite. And my ass is not fat.

The second was Tasha. But it was Chi who leaped forward to help me up. Nick was too smashed to do much of anything except clutch me with his eyes closed. Maybe he had passed out.

"Gen, what are you doing? I thought you didn't like Nick anymore!" Chi said as he pulled the limbo stick off us and lifted me to my feet. His expression was hurt and angry. "I thought Nick was a big mistake."

I was totally stunned but managed to squeak out, "I'm not with Nick, I swear. This was all an accident."

Stupid Nick just lay there grinning on the sand-covered floor. He was too wasted to figure out what was going on yet.

"A total accident," I repeated for good measure.

The room had gone deathly silent. Everyone was watching with eager eyes, including the guys who'd been holding the limbo stick. I swear you could have heard a pin drop.

"You lying phony," CJ said, snarling in my face. She was white as a sheet but managed to look like a model in her gold thong bikini. "I should have listened when you said you were a slut, because you are one. A total slut."

"You've got a nerve, CJ Thompson," I snarled right back. "I'm not the one who goes through guys like Kleenex." I was breathing really fast and the room spun around, but I wasn't going to take any of her crap.

CJ's eyes turned to slits. "What? You can't talk to me like that when I found you dry-humping my boyfriend."

"Nick and I were doing the limbo, and only because he made me," I continued. "It's not my fault you can't control your men."

"You bitch," she spat. "You're so pathetic—climbing all over a guy just to get him to like you."

I really don't like people crowding me.

"Hey, wait a sec, CJ," Chi said, stepping between us. "You've got no right to rag on Genesis. Nick's the one you should be mad at. He's the player, not her." At least he believed me.

CJ snorted and opened her mouth to reply, but Tasha was suddenly right next to us.

"How would *you* know?" Tasha burst out, grabbing Chi by the arm. Tasha's trips to the spray-on tanning booth worked, because her white suit looked great against her fake-bronzed skin. "Why are you defending her, anyway?"

"Isn't it obvious? She must be doing your boyfriend, too," CJ said.

Tasha sunk her nails into Chi. "He wouldn't do that. He's crazy about me. Aren't you, Chi?"

People were now whispering and giggling, but everyone was still watching us. Like we were a movie.

"Gen and I are *good* friends," Chi said. "I care a lot about her, though. She's an awesome person."

I noticed he didn't exactly answer Tasha's question. Tasha noticed too.

"Don't you love me anymore? Are you breaking up with me?" She was more shocked than upset.

Chi shrugged. "I thought *you* were breaking up with me. I thought you had someone new."

Tasha gaped at him. "Um, I'm sorry, Chi. I was going to tell you everything . . . honest." Then she stared at the ground. "It's not like I don't like you."

Nick finally stumbled to his feet and shoved the bar to the side. "Hey, Chi, my man, sounds like you really *are* hot for Genesis," he said. He looked at me with drunken puppy-dog eyes. "But, Gen, what about *us*?"

Omigod. I couldn't believe this. "There *is* no us," I said. "You're with CJ, remember?"

"Not anymore," CJ huffed. She was really pissed. She knew every girl in the room was gloating over her embarrassment. Even the guys were grinning and nudging each other. She couldn't take it. "I have a new man. A real man. He's not some high school kid." She tossed her head.

Nick looked at CJ and then at me. "Women. Shit. I don't need this." He hiccupped and looked down at his shorts, which were leaking. "Shit, my bottle of Finito broke too." He looked more upset over losing his hangover preventive than over losing CJ. He hiccupped again and staggered off with wet sand clinging to the back of his shorts.

Tash was staring at Chi.

"We're not really finished, are we?" Tasha asked him. "We can still hang out together, right? At least as friends?"

"Sure," Chi said gently. He was so sweet. He couldn't be mean to Tasha, even though he knew she deserved it.

CJ spun around and glared at me. "All I know is that someone needs to kick Miss Homewrecker's ass." She puffed up her scrawny body and shook a fist at me.

That was it. I'm not Angela Bell's daughter for nothing. I outweigh CJ by at least twenty pounds. I took two steps toward her.

"Go ahead, CJ," I said. "Bring it on."

I must have looked pretty menacing.

"You don't scare me, Genesis," CJ bluffed.

"Right," I said, and smiled at her.

CJ sputtered and cursed but backed away. I could have flattened her without straining a muscle.

Here's a really good reason why being superskinny isn't so great: it makes it too easy for normal-sized people to whup your ass.

CJ and I stood for a second, sizing each other up. She blinked first.

"I'm outta here. Breathing the same air as you losers is making me sick," she growled, glaring at Chi and me. "Tasha, c'mon."

Tasha followed, looking a little dazed and confused. "Bye, Chi," she called out. She didn't say a word to me.

Someone applauded; then someone else joined in. Soon every girl in the room was clapping. "Way to go, Genesis!" someone shouted.

Message Board

✉ <u>!!!</u>—007UGO—at 7:32 p.m.
Omigod {8-O what a nightmare! I would have died.

✉ <u>Re: !!!</u>—JUICYFRUIT45—at 7:54 p.m.
Me too!

✉ <u>Re: !!!</u>—QueenSheba—at 7:59 p.m.
i totally agree. it doesn't get worse than that! time to leave town.

MOST RECENT ENTRIES   CALENDAR

VIEW FRIENDS   LINKS   PHOTOS

19/04 12:01:00

CONFESSIONS OF A BOYFRIEND STEALER—
BLOG BY GENESIS BELL

[21ST ENTRY]

Guess what? I didn't want to die or leave town. It was a really bad scene, but I was okay. Maybe because I was producing a TV show and had to act like a professional, or maybe because I was just ready for this ultimate Terrible showdown. I don't know.

I was all alone in a room full of people who were whispering, snickering, and staring at me. A few girls came up to shake my hand, but I really wanted everyone to just move on.

Tasha and CJ had left (no way would they stick around the party after that major embarrassment). Nick was nowhere to be seen. Chi had stuck around for a few seconds but then decided he should go talk to Tasha. I assured him I was okay and everything was under control. He agreed but kept staring at me over his shoulder as he walked away.

I was freaked out by it all, to say the least, but as they say, the show must go on. People were still standing around, which wasn't a good thing, cinema-wise.

"Guys, let's get back to partying, okay?" My voice only shook a little as I spoke to my audience. "I'm here to film a Fiesta Beach documentary, not the Genesis Bell soap opera."

There was a brief silence, but then everyone got the message. They drifted back to doing whatever it was they'd been doing before.

One girl I didn't recognize came up to me and said, "I wanted to say that you're my hero," and walked away, but that was it. Someone cranked up the music and people started dancing, drinking, and making out—typical party stuff.

I knew that I had to comment about the limbo incident, but I was too shaken up to be all clever and insightful about it.

"Obviously, this producer didn't plan on being in the middle of a catfight. Let's analyze that little smackdown later, okay?" I tried to sound serious and professional.

I was damned if I'd let CJ and Tasha ruin my big chance at the career of my dreams. I was shaking for a while, but over the next hour, I was relieved to see that the party was back to normal. Yeah, I know people were still gossiping like crazy, but I got some great shots of people dirty dancing. I also filmed a bunch of football players and cheerleaders in the Jacuzzi watching *The Wizard of Oz* on a big-screen TV. Some of the football players were reciting all the lines along with the characters.

I did not take any shots of Nick and Sherryn Feldman slow-dancing drunkenly on top of the expensive-looking suede love seat. Nick still had sand on his trunks, by the way.

But Fiesta Beach, party of the year, came to an untimely end around midnight. Mr. and Mrs. Fortis showed up unexpectedly and staggered into the house laden with suitcases. It was supposed to be a big surprise for Andy, and believe me, it was. They seemed only mildly surprised to walk into this huge party, but they probably knew their son pretty well. They didn't even get upset, but everyone, including me, scattered like someone had dropped a nuke-sized stink bomb. I was disappointed but also relieved. I really needed to go home and unwind. I needed to think. I needed a break.

Message Board

✉ Re: !!! — 007UGO — at 11:12 P.M.
Okay, I really want to see Genesis's documentary now!

✉ Re: !!! — JUICYFRUIT45 — at 11:42 P.M.
Arrrgh! I wish I could see it, but guess I'm out of luck unless you guys send me a DVD copy . . . or maybe if MTV puts it on air.

✉= Re: !!!—QueenSheba—at 11:50 p.m.

i guess genesis's film will kind of show the truth. should we believe her side or not? her documentary should tell us.

✉= Re: !!!—007ugo—at 12:01 a.m.

I don't know. I think genesis's blog has been pretty honest. She is lucky because her life is never boring (like mine!) ☺

MOST RECENT ENTRIES   CALENDAR
VIEW FRIENDS   LINKS   PHOTOS

20/04 09:06:55

CONFESSIONS OF A BOYFRIEND STEALER—
BLOG BY GENESIS BELL

[22ND ENTRY]

If I'd made anything up, I would have cut all the embarrassing parts out. Right? This is a totally true confession. But wait, there's more. My story didn't end just yet.

← →

I was so tired I could barely hold on to my duffel bag. Man, did I need to go to bed.

It was all hitting me at once. Thoughts were racing through my head about CJ, Tasha, Nick, Chi, Fiesta Beach, and my documentary. I staggered into the living room and nearly ran right back outside.

My mother was screaming, "Traitor! I'm surrounded by dirty-dog traitors! My own child who I breast-fed for three months, even though it meant I had to get implants later on in life!"

She was kicking her statue of the shepherds and

lambs around the living room. One lamb head flew off and missed hitting my stomach by inches.

Crap. I'd walked into yet another trauma-drama scene.

"I can't believe I raised a Jezebel!" my mother panted. *Bam!* There went another lamb's head. *Bam!* The shepherds rolled several feet and went right under the coffee table.

I couldn't have said anything if I'd tried. Shay and Kenny? Omigod. Yeah, my sister was capable of pulling stunts like this (so was Angela). Deep down, I'd guessed Shay might be up to something stupid like going after Kenny, but I didn't want to admit it to myself, because that meant I'd have to deal with it.

Just then, my sister raced up and grabbed one of the lamb's heads and hurled it against the wall. "And I can't believe my own mother would be so mean to me! I never even slept with him!"

I cowered in the doorway. The two of them going nuts wasn't a pretty sight.

"You spent the day with Kenny at his spiritual retreat! He never took me there once!" Angela's voice rose in outrage. "And I had to wait all day and night till you two came back home!"

"It was his cabin on the lake, Mother, which you wouldn't go to because it didn't have air-conditioning, and anyway, we were just *talking.* Like I've told you a million times!"

Angela sucked in a huge breath. "Hah! You mean

you waited till you got back to his house to make your move! We're going to keep at it till I get the truth!"

"I just gave him a teensy kiss, and he pushed me away. He loves you. He was being nice to me because I said I needed help. Religious help."

I stared at Shay; she had to be kidding.

"You expect me to believe that? You two were sneaking around behind my back!"

Maybe Angela did love Kenny. Staking out his house all day and night was so un-Angela-like. I've never seen her so upset. Damn, I really had fallen down on the job. A bouncer isn't supposed to take her eye off the crowd for a second. My head started to ache.

Shay shot back with the typical kid's response: "No one understands me!"

My mother suddenly noticed me standing there. She charged across the room and got right in my face.

"Your sister, Shay Bell," she said, grabbing my shoulder really hard, "your sister, Shay Bell, has stolen my Kenny, the only man I've ever loved."

Shay rushed over and grabbed my other shoulder. "Don't listen to her, Gen. Kenny wouldn't even kiss me back. I didn't mean anything. I just got carried away—"

"She planned the whole thing. She was going to se-duce my Kenny. My own daughter—my own flesh and blood," my mother spat out.

"I just didn't want anyone to know I was talking with Kenny. He's the one who felt all guilty about it, even though we didn't do anything wrong." Shay shot Angela a wounded look.

I knew Shay didn't want Kenny for herself; Shay was a hunk-o-holic. A guy had to be a nine to have a chance with her. . . . And she hated anything that threatened the Angela-Shay Club. This was the collagen lip thing all over again. Shay had to be number one with Angela.

"You wanted to trap him. Admit it," Angela said.

I suddenly realized that my shoulders really hurt. Neither of them was letting go.

"But I didn't do anything," Shay whined. "I was going to apologize to Kenny when you jumped us."

"I saw them, Genesis," my mother said. "On the porch. Shay's lips touching Kenny's. I'll never get over it." She covered her eyes dramatically. "To think if I hadn't parked down the street and hid in the bushes, I'd have never found out the truth."

Omigod, Angela was a stalker. I took that moment to pull away and step back a good few yards.

"No one understands me," Shay whimpered again. "I was feeling really down about my life and stuff." She wiped her eyes and sniffed. "And now you'll be mad at me forever. I didn't mean it. I didn't."

She began to cry, and so did my mother. Omigod. My head ached even more. But this wasn't serious, I reminded myself. This was just my family.

"You'll always be my baby girl, Shay," Angela said in a much softer voice. "I've made mistakes too. I know you didn't mean to kiss Kenny."

They threw their arms around each other. "We'll work it out," Angela said. "Maybe you, me, and Kenny can sit down and talk. Maybe the Lord will help us, especially now that Kenny's divorce is final."

Oh no. Angela was dragging poor God into it.

I've witnessed this sort of scene before (minus the religious stuff). My mother and sister have to stir up drama every couple of months. Normally I'd have spent the next hour making sure they stayed calm (and sane), but not this time. I just wanted to escape to my room. I deserved some peace.

My sister and mother both shrieked when they saw me walking out of the living room. "Genesis, where do you think you're going? How can you leave us now?"

I paused. "You guys will be okay. You always are."

"How can you say that? We're in a *crisis*," Shay blared.

"Well, guess what, so am *I*." The words dropped like bombs. I was shocked that I was saying them.

Angela and Shay stared at me like I was insane. Maybe I was. Maybe I didn't care.

I heard myself say, "I just had one of the most amazing nights of my life. I've probably lost my best friends. I've probably broken up their relationships with their boyfriends. I've probably started a real career in television. I've probably made Jamaica Plains High history." I stopped to catch my breath. Surprisingly, my headache was almost gone, and I wasn't so tired. I felt like a huge weight had been lifted. "Um, I guess that's it—for now."

My sister and mother continued to stare. Their mouths had dropped open.

"Good night," I said.

MESSAGE BOARD

✉ I TAKE BACK WHAT I SAID—007ugo—AT 6:21 A.M.

I think I'd rather have a blah life than have to deal with genesis's family. can you imagine finding out that your mom and sister were into the same man? Ugh . . . too Anna Nicole. Poor Genesis!

✉ Re: I TAKE BACK WHAT I SAID—Queen-Sheba—AT 7:01 A.M.

she should have made a documentary about her family! they are totally weird people. i'd go mental if i had to live with them.

✉ Re: I TAKE BACK WHAT I SAID—JUICYFRUIT45—AT 7:23 A.M.

I know, but genesis seemed to handle it. I think she's a cool person. I was sooo freaked out by Shay. i thought she was just being a brat. I didn't think she would go after her mom's boyfriend. But you know what? Genesis is totally not like her family.

✉ <u>Re: I Take Back What I Said</u>—OO7U90—at 7:45 a.m.

I was so glad that Genesis blasted her mom and sister. I bet she shocked them. Maybe they finally got a clue about genesis and everything. Maybe they finally woke up and decided to be a better family.

MOST RECENT ENTRIES   CALENDAR

VIEW FRIENDS   LINKS   PHOTOS

`21/04 07:12:22`

CONFESSIONS OF A BOYFRIEND STEALER—
BLOG BY GENESIS BELL

[23RD ENTRY]

After their initial shock, Angela and Shay got over my outburst. They decided I was going through a "phase." What they don't know is that my phase will probably last forever, or close to it.

← →

The Fiesta Beach documentary is going to be a huge success, but . . . I had to cut out the limbo incident. I know that sucks, but CJ threatened to sue me and the school. Her dad had the money and connections to make everyone sweat, and the principal totally freaked. He begged me to cut the sequence, so I did. I wasn't even allowed to *describe* the limbo incident. I knew if we got sued Angela would drag us all to *Judge Judy,* and I dreaded the very thought of it.

I made sure to say on film that I'd been forced to edit out an important moment between me and my ex–best friends because one ex–best friend was threatening to sue. A good producer knows how to deliver a message even when her hands are tied.

CJ didn't win, though, trust me. Next month, everyone is going to watch the Fiesta Beach documentary on the big screen in the auditorium. They're gonna love it, I know it. I captured the real stuff. The good stuff. The down-and-dirty teen stuff. Maybe the film was too gritty and too revealing in places, but it's gonna rock the house.

Oh yeah, Andy Fortis didn't get in trouble with his parents; they were thrilled that their house was filmed and were hoping HGTV might want to do a special on it.

Mr. Nichols watched the documentary and said it broke new ground. He said I did an amazing job (he gave me an A-plus).

I've gotten friendly with Cher and a few other girls in media class, but we're not exactly soul sisters. At least not yet. Maybe never.

The Terrible Three have disbanded. I've been kicked out, anyway. I see Tash and CJ all the time, so they're the Terrible Two now. When our paths do cross, CJ and I exchange hateful looks; Tasha and I avoid looking at each other altogether. CJ and Dave, the Fresh Squeeze Palace guy, are an official item—for now. As if I care.

Chi and Tash said they'd be friends, but they've really drifted apart. Tash is too busy with her new guy, Chad. I know Chi still has feelings for me, but I told him we need to be cool for a long while. I don't want to be his rebound girl or Tasha's follow-up act. We hang out at Dog Eat Dog and talk. He watched my Fiesta Beach show, though, and told me it was really brilliant. He was pissed that I had to cut the limbo incident. He's so supportive.

Nick still e-mails and IMs me from time to time, but I don't take it seriously. He's not with Sherryn Feldman. He's not pining over CJ either, that's for sure. I guess he's playing the field. I swear I saw him with that chick with the major roots from the Blue Circle. Big surprise.

I do miss hanging out with CJ and Tash. We had our good times—going on Hottie Patrols at the mall, sneaking backstage at concerts, pretending to be rich and famous, and shaking things up in general. I have to admit that the Terribles made life kind of exciting. It sucks at times not being one of them. I mean, you get used to being part of something, and then, *bam!*, you're out in the cold. But I'm getting over it. Guess I'll have to make my own excitement.

This summer I may be going to New York to intern for a new cable network called Kick TV. It's supposed to be "teen centered" and very hip. Andy Fortis's dad knows someone, and he thinks he can get me in. I'm psyched. I'd be escaping everything here—memories of CJ and Tasha—and the Bell household. Speaking of which . . .

I know you're wondering about the Shay, Kenny,

and Angela drama. Well, they're all in counseling with Kenny's pastor. I know, I know. How freaky can you get, especially after Shay tried to seduce Kenny. I mean, a woman and her daughter going after the same guy? You might be shocked, but sad to say, I'm not. I try not to let them drive me nuts, because what else can I do? Someday I'll have a very different life, but until then, I gotta cope.

I think Kenny realizes he'll have to play second fiddle to Shay and Angela's relationship, but I guess he doesn't care. He's totally crazy about Angela, or maybe just totally crazy. I don't mind having him around. He does bring good takeout, and maybe he can be the new bouncer of the Bell household.

I can hope.

I'm ready for New York, and who knows where after that. Maybe Toronto or L.A. I know I won't be the Jan Brady of Jamaica Plains anymore.

As for this blog, I guess I should say goodbye for now. Or as they say in the movie biz, that's a wrap . . . unless something else comes up.

MESSAGE BOARD

✉ OMIGOD! YOU GUYS, WAIT TILL YOU HEAR!—JUICYFRUIT45—9:45 A.M.
Hey!!! I heard that CJ's blog is online!!!! It may just be a rumor, because no one has the actual link. But I am DYING to read it. I'll keep you posted. ☺

✉ **OMIGOD! YOU GUYS, WAIT TILL YOU HEAR!**—007U90—9:57 a.m.

OMIGOD! (:-O Genesis was smart to get her blog out first! Let us know when you get the info, juicyfruit45.

✉ **OMIGOD! YOU GUYS, WAIT TILL YOU HEAR!**—QUEENSHEBA—10:01 a.m.

yeah, juicyfruit45, you HAVE TO KEEP US POSTED! cj probably has a lot to say! bet she's read genesis's blog and is pissed. genesis better watch out!